The Race
Is Not
Given

11/1/2020

To Susan —

The Race
Is Not
Given

Frank Dobson

Thank you –

Peace and

Blessings,

Frank

D

Pittsburgh, PA

ISBN 1-56315-194-4

Paperback Fiction
© Copyright 1999 Frank Dobson
All rights reserved
First Printing—1999
Library of Congress #98-85361

Request for information should be addressed to:

SterlingHouse Publisher, Inc.
The Sterling Building
440 Friday Road
Department T-101
Pittsburgh, PA 15209

Cover design & Typesetting: Drawing Board Studios

This is a work of fiction. Names, characters, places, and incidents either are the
product of the author's imagination or are used fictitiously. Any resemblance to
actual events or persons, living or dead is entirely coincidental.

Printed in Canada

To My Parents
With Love

Part I

Ecclessiates 9:11

I returned and I saw
under the sun, that the race
is not given to the swift,
nor the battle to the strong . . .
but time and chance happens to them all.

CHAPTER
1
I Returned

Naked, he ran hard. The black cinder track sizzled, like the hot iron skillet when his momma fried bacon. The stadium was full with faces he knew. His momma, pretty brown, smiling tensely through fears that her baby might not make it. Bro Max, bragging, talkin' trash, like he was back home, holding court on the streets of Freeport. 'Ton and KK, cheering, raising their fists, urging him on. Sheila, Maxi and Leah were there too, laughing, mocking, or seeming to pretend he wasn't there, sweatin' like hell, haulin' ass. His father was absent.

He always awoke from the dream dripping with sweat and burning or bone dry and cold. Afterwards, regardless of the time of night, he couldn't return to sleep. He'd sit up in his bed. Write in his journal or pen a letter to Max or Sheila—a letter that could never be sent, in either case. Max, his best friend, track team partner and rival, was dead. Sheila, his ex-wife, was somewhere on the planet; where, he didn't know. They'd "lost touch with each other," her choice. Afterwards, he hummed songs about running. From childhood: "Run, run, as fast as you can, you can't catch me, I'm the Gingerbread Man." From church: "Lord, I'm runnin', tryin' to make a hundred, ninety-nine and a half won't do." From Max's beloved Bahamas: "We rushin', we rushin', we rushin' through the crowd. We rushin', we rushin', we standin' tall 'n proud." Afterwards, he'd close his eyes, and sing softly, like his momma used to do. He'd imitate a soul singer, Al Green, Billy Paul, Marvin Gaye, someone from the seventies, ten, twelve years ago, and remember a party, a date, a good time, and then be glad he'd come home. Home. Nowhere else he ever lived was home, not the two years in Nebraska following college; not the three in Cali with Sheila; not the several after that, by himself, in PA. Nowhere else he'd ever been, or would ever be, was home, but here, his hometown, Buffalo, NY. No other house but this one, 253 Mason Avenue, felt right all the time, even when things, like now, were wrong. Nowhere else could he awake from his nightmares and so readily remember good things; nowhere else could he run from them and forget why he returned home.

He was diagnosed with cancer. Dr. Parker, his first doctor in Harrisburg said, "I'm going to be straight with you, big fella. The cancer is possibly terminal. There's a 50-50 chance. We can try to burn or poison it out, and after that, there's nothing more we can do." So, he took the treatments. Radiation. Chemo. Burning out the disease, poisoning it. Taking the treatments, for months at a time, sickened him, weakened him. It just wasn't about losing his hair or sense of taste or appetite. And, it just wasn't about dropping 55 pounds during four months of treatment, so that he was made weak not simply from the radiation or the drugs, but from a less fit body than he before he began. It was about taking treatments so he could die. The first time he walked into the hospital's radiation room, he was greeted by 10, 15 other patients, all raising their heads upwards, in unison, as another walking wounded joined the company. They were surrounded by a cloud of smoke, heavy, like the fog of a dreary morning. When he said to the woman sitting next to him, awaiting treatment, that smoking is bad for your health, she replied dryly, "What difference does it make now, anyway, sugar?" It was as though the patients submitted to the burning, cutting, or poisoning of the cancer without any real belief that it would work. His doctor was right, "50-50." Then Stan found Dr. Goldstein, an expert in chemo, and this treatment wiped out the disease totally, or so they thought. But recently, the cancer returned. Stan obeyed, and went back into treatment. Journeyed back to the place, the awful place, where he felt betrayed by his body, but betrayed also, by the treatment to cure his body. And so, after months of more treatment, in this the second year of his life with cancer, a horrible marriage with no possibility of divorce, he began to question the doctors. Not that what they were doing was wrong, but that perhaps, there was a better way, a way which was more right for him. He read everything on health and nutrition and drugs. But he'd stopped working out. Stopped, because he lacked the strength to do so. And then, one day, he began experimenting with herbs and vitamins, based on his reading, trying, "here a little, there a little," like Elder Mitchell, his father's pastor, preached. He began to work out again, the same as when he was in school, walking the distances he used to run; decreasing the weight lifted in half, but doing the same old things again. He persisted with the cancer treatments, but they didn't make him feel as bad as before. He felt better, felt, not that the doctors failed, but that he was succeeding. It was wild, this cancer. Getting this dreaded disease opened him up to a new side of life, of living. Perhaps the fear of death gave him greater courage to live. And so he decided to move back home. Not just to get away from Goldstein and the treatments which he was going to try to live, or die, without, but also because he could find there, in his parents' house, what no other place in America could offer him, another culture, another country. When he contracted the disease, was informed of it, he thought long and hard about how it happened to him: heredity, environment, habit? He didn't know. In part, he blamed the culture. In part, he blamed the dog-eat-dog way he lived his life, especially after Sheila, trying to best, compete with, his vanished ex-wife. He wanted to better her so she could see, in her absence, his worth. It was like buying a present for a dead person. Worse. The job in Harrisburg was a result of this attitude, Assistant Director to the President of a program for wayward, poor, "at-risk" youth. It was the type of job where, if he played his politics right, he would eventually move up. And if he didn't, he would be able to move out, into another similar program, as president or director, as big-money head. They hired him because of his track background, figuring it would impress the kids; and also, Stan thought, because they couldn't afford to hire a bigger-name ex-jock. But he left the job and the future and even, in some way, the present, and entered into a timeless zone, where jobs and money didn't matter. The future didn't matter. Nothing mattered but his plan for the future, a future he calculated second by precious second. He returned home, to the culture, the country of his parents' house, he dared not call it a home, because here, he could work his plan and not worry about money or time. He took a major cut in pay, approximately 20,000 dollars, but that didn't bother him, really, he didn't need that much money anyway. It was crazy, what he was doing, leaving the advice of the experts, the physicians, and going on his own. But weren't they the ones who informed him, once he began working out his own cure, that "you look better, Stan; you seem to be taking to the treatments this time." But it wasn't their treatments; it was his: ginseng and bee pollen and vitamins and royal jelly and distilled water and other herbs. It wasn't their treatments; it was a change in lifestyle—a questioning of everything, from where he worked—he hated the job, anyway, the politics of it; the only part he missed was the kids—to what he ate. He studied the label of everything he ate; prepared almost everything he ate; and seemed almost crazy, to himself, in his obsession. But it was like he was taking on the culture, a cancerous culture, really, one in which it was a surprise that everybody didn't contract the disease. It was no surprise to him that black men were a leading group of cancer sufferers. His plan was to hone his body into such good shape, that it would fight the cancer, the same kind of shape it was in when he ran track. He aimed to prove them wrong—the doctors and all of those in the stadium of his nightmares. The doctors were right, his nightmares said, just like other naysayers were right about his life, his dreams. The doctors were wrong, his life and breath said. He returned home to die; no, rather, he returned home to live. The doctors didn't think it was possible. How did they know what was possible? He quit his job in Harrisburg and came home.

Piles of leaves—orange, yellow, green leaves, hit the air and settled. Sunday morning, 9:00 am., October, Stan was in his sweats and tennis shoes, walking street curbs, kicking leaves. He'd come out to run. His body desired a run, to take the block in five minutes flat. Stan's father, Richard, was at church. Richard superintended as well as taught Sunday School, ushered, and deaconed. Most Sundays, son and father, Stan and Richard, awoke at the same time. The father's alarm, set only and always on Saturday nights for Sunday mornings, always for the same time, 7:00 am.; and always, it sounded twice—two beeps before his father rolled over or rose up to stop the sound, for he invariably slept on the same side of the bed, near the nightstand and, invariably, the brief sound awakened the son.

A typical Sunday morning, so typical of the way things were for Stan the past seven months, since his return. The inhabitants of the house refused to speak to each other, unless they absolutely had to. They never spoke with their hearts, only their heads—pleasantries and politenesses which must be said, regardless. "Did you pay this bill?" "Can you drop by the store for that?" "So and so called for you at such and such a time." Years ago, Sunday mornings were different, full of activity and big breakfasts—grits, eggs, pancakes, the works—while they joyously scurried about to leave together for the house of the Lord. But now, his father traveled alone. This particular morning, before he left, Stan and he talked. He opened Stan's bedroom door. He was dressed in a black, double-breasted suit, with white shirt, black tie. The tips of his black dress boots shone. His trench coat was open, its belt buckled in back. He stood in Stan's room, one hand holding his briefcase and the other the doorknob. Stan had listened for forty-five minutes to the movements of the man facing him. His father's walking in and out of the bedroom, his father's showering, shaving, primping—he listened and waited for his father to come to him.

* * * * *

"Morning," Stan spoke first.

"You make sure your mom don't go out today. I'm staying at church for supper." As he spoke, Richard looked first at the white wall in back of Stan's bed, then at his son's lean, muscular brown body beneath the white sheet. He wanted to remove the sheet, at least partially, to see better the man that he and Nancy turned out. For a moment, he tried to place the man, to take the man back. And looking made him hate, for a second, this man, his son. He knew that long, long ago he lost his wife, his son. His son wanted nothing from him, and the space between them, as he stood three feet from the bed where Stan lay, seemed to hold the reason why. His son seemed at that moment like a lover, someone with whom one has slept and afterwards wonders why, and afterwards abhors. The connection between them escaped him. Richard wanted to change whatever it was that governed their relationship, to find and force it to change. He stood in the doorway for two, three minutes, saying nothing, simply staring. He was caught; so Stan's reply, not content but the sound, startled him.

"Yeah. Good."

"Bye, see you later."

He released the doorknob and left, leaving his son's door ajar.

* * * * *

After his father left, Stan arose. On his way downstairs, he paused by his mother's door—she was sleeping heavily. If he didn't wake her, there was no telling how long she would remain in bed. Once up, she would go to the bathroom and urinate—hard, fast, audible though the bathroom door was shut. And this particular morning, as he was kicking leaves, Stan thought of his mother and started to run faster. While she was in bed with a hang-over from the night before, his father was in church saying his prayers. It was quiet as he ran. He worked out on Sunday mornings until the corner drugstore opened, at 10:00 a.m. Then he would get his Sunday paper, which would occupy him for the remainder of the morning. Some Sundays, it seemed to him as though the surrounding world were his, only his. It was a black working-class world, composed of old one-family dwellings and duplexes with awninged porches and tiny front lawns. It was reckless tots and cranky old folks who together owned the sidewalk; it was plethoric young people who alone ruled the street. Stan was raised in this world, this neighborhood, lived much of his life calling the same house home, the same street his and, for the most part, the same faces neighbors. None he grew up with went bad in the usual sense of the term when it's used about blacks. Almost everyone screwed, smoked, or stole *some*; and others went to jail for relatively insignificant crimes, petty theft, or died before their proverbial time, but no big-time pimps, whorish, uncaring mothers or cold killers roamed the neighborhood backyards with him. None made good in the stereotypical ways reserved, in some minds, for black folk. The prettiest, most effervescent girls, were lured, not by Hollywood or Motown, but by another man, to another bed. And, perhaps, another black baby was born. The strongest boys, with the sharpest shots, hadn't, from this neighborhood, made the pros. No, the best and brightest from his childhood had not ventured to their lands of heart's desire, but settled instead for Bethlehem Steel and Buffalo Forge. (Stan wondered if they tried.) His old playmates were now hard-working men whose talk centered around such subjects as the fortunes of the local football team, the Bills, and getting enough overtime during a certain week so as to double up on the car or house payments. They were once fly, sharp young girls who now and then captured, on a blessed weekend, a painted and pinched image of their former selves; once pretty women whose talk now was who recently married for the second or third time and how so and so looked. Those who did good, made it, did so in a small way. And those who fared poorly, went bad, did so by simply working wrong, loving wrong, perhaps even dreaming wrong. None gained notoriety. The tragedies and the successes of this world were unspectacular, silent, like its Sunday mornings. And so Stan ran, not because he was the hope of his old friends and neighbors, even though he, more than they, came so close to "making it." He ran because he was his own last hope, and running was something that he, a former track star, still did well, in spite of his illness. He didn't run to keep the old neighborhood alive—there was no way he could kill it. He ran in order to use it.

* * * * *

Nancy overheard her husband and son talking to one another. A few words, just a couple by each, then silence, then Richard's steps past her door. A mother cannot be ambivalent about her child, nor can she be ambivalent towards the man whose seed helped produce that child. Nancy Thompson covered her head with her pillow to insure that she didn't hear what they said. She imagined that the sounds she heard contained the words "son," "father." And the loud steps past her door weren't steps at all, and her husband, who hadn't slept with her, loved her in over two years, was beside her, his head nuzzled into her breasts.

She told herself that her husband was a good man, a man living for God. She still regarded him as her man. At times, she knew, the individuals in this house lived as though they were the only persons in the world. Even she. Because she must. But she never forgot the men in her life. Even when she went out to get drunk, she spoke of herself as mother, infrequently spoke of herself as wife, but mother, she was that, and when she drank, that became her obsession. At "The Black Bar" or "B.B.'s," where she went to drink, she was referred to not as Nancy or Mrs. Thompson, but as "Stan's mom," and she played it to the max.

"Yeah, you bet I am his mom. Stanford Michael Thompson, young lady, that big pretty negro you see running around your block." Or, "my Stan's a top athlete, conference 400 meter champ his last two years in college. Yeah, that's his picture Johnny's got up there behind the bar."

She was a proud woman who reveled in appearances. Tall, statuesque, of a reddish-brown complexion. Grey hair trimmed in a neat Afro style. She loved being offered a light, a drink, no matter if the offerer were female or male. She loved to tell tales. At B.B.'s they were mainly tales of her son, his feats. At home, Stan was audience, not subject. She believed one should have few secrets from one's seed. Much of the time, it was the same old story. She felt, throughout the years, the repeated tellings and retellings, that perhaps she only related bits, pieces, but she prayed that to him it was full, clear.

Her first husband dead. And afterwards, the feeling that she hadn't done him right. "Yeah, we were young. I was young. He went to Korea, came back, and was killed just walking down the street. I don't know if I was a good wife to Roy. I was just 20 when we got married in 1948. But you got to remember that he was away from me for two of those years. I was crazy back then, though. We was crazy. Rented an apartment in Brooklyn, on Dekalb Avenue, and when he left for Korea, Roy told me to stay put, make sure I kept that apartment. Wanted to be certain of one thing, where I was. And I did—stay put. In more ways than one. I loved that man, but when he returned to me, all the craziness, the magic was gone. For five months, before he passed, Roy and I did three things together. Eat breakfast, make love, and go to the movies on Saturday afternoons. Your daddy, Stan, he was different. He came along the year after Roy was killed. Seemed like he might be able to make me forget. Can't nobody make a person forget somebody they need to remember. And I needed to remember so much about Roy. But your daddy was so fine. I mean, he was a good looking man. Dressed at least as sharp as he does today. No money, sometimes no job, but sharp. Like he was determined to impress the world. And he walked, strutted, like the whole damn world was going to watch him. I felt that anybody looking that good was going places. He said law school. But no matter what, he never looked sad or sorry, like so many of our men back then."

She told Stan at an early age because she felt he could handle it. And the boy grew up with a sensitivity that she made, knowing, feeling things as she gave. It was a soft circle, her creation. He was always her bright boy, the best, and she lavished on him what she could not give his father. From the beginning Richard called it spoiling the boy, giving him a false idea of how the world worked and said the world was not going to view him the way she did. Yet Nancy was steadfast. She possessed something special, and the world could not tell her different. She experienced this feeling before, first with Roy. With him, it was a shared thing, them together. Him alone, no. But with her, he perked. . . . Richard. He was, in her words, "so dog-gone majestic" that she could not resist, nor could she actually believe he wanted her. Yet nothing became hers. He simply showed himself in all his glory. It was still, and had always been, his for him alone. But then, her son. She carried, gave birth to, him and the specialness was there. At first, it frightened her. And she would weep when she brushed the child's hair or fussed with his clothes. Perhaps this was because she knew how much like the father he loathed, even as a child, the son was. Later, though, it made her proud. Perhaps this was because she, so close, saw uniqueness as only a loving and nurturing eye can see, 'til that uniqueness—a mole, an eyelash—beautiful because unique to the loved one, blooms beauty which the world, too, cannot help but see. Yes, she knew what she had. But whereas with Roy she afterwards blamed herself for the loss, and with Richard she faulted herself for even having tried, with Stan she was determined not to lose. He was her son, and that gave her rights and a part of this man that she as wife never really owned.

* * * * *

Stan ended his run at the steps of P.S. #6, his old grammar school. He ran daily. On alternate days, he lifted weights. Today, after he finished reading the paper, he would run two miles to the university to work in the weight room. His body was in good shape. The cold, damp morning concrete felt hard against his buttocks. Its hardness was to him an affirmation of his own.

As he sat he did isometrics. His arms were bent at right angles, his forearms in front of his chest, his palms meeting, and his fingers pointed upward. The pressure of one arm against the other. He did this exercise compulsively. At the shoestore, while waiting for customers to come in or to make up their minds, he would do this. Customers would sometimes eye him curiously, but he ignored them. What others thought, said, did, mattered about as much as this old school building meant to him after he graduated. Not even Leah, the woman, no, in his mind, girl, he slept with, held him. He tried; and he laughed as he thought of it, giving himself to others: his father, Sheila. It didn't work. But part of him said he couldn't give up. It was about patience. And living each day as if it were his last, like when he tried out for the high school team. Over the course of a summer, he worked his "heart, head, and ass off," in Coach Crestman's words, to go from "fourth-best 800 meters runner to best 400 meters runner in the school's history." He got up from the steps of the school. He was on his way to the drugstore and then home.

Nancy shouted from upstairs as soon as he entered the house, "Leah called! You hear me, Stan? Come here for a minute." He climbed the stairs to her bedroom and entered. She was in bed, sitting up, watching television. A rainbow of plump, colorful pillows decorated the head of the bed and supported her. "Come here give me a kiss," she said.

He sat down on the edge of the bed, leaned over, and kissed her cheek.

"Mm-good. That'll make my day." She smiled, paused, took a sip from the strong-smelling ebony coffee which was in a cup on a nightstand next to the bed. "So, how's my man today?" she asked, replacing the cup on the nightstand.

She had referred to him as "my man" for so long—at least back to when he first knew what the term meant. During boyhood, when he came home from school or play, the words encouraged him. But today he closed his eyes at the sound. Shook his head at the sound. Leaned back against the head of the bed and wanted to weep. To ask her why, why, weren't things right? She was his mother, his still pretty mom, his beautiful mom who possessed a voice, a rap, a song that could mesmerize, a smile that was light—why, then, he wanted to cry, weren't things right? And when he opened his eyes, he simply stared at the wall facing them.

* * * * *

Nancy was praying to herself. She placed her hand over his and spoke audibly. "Lord, give us life. True peace. Bless this day in our hearts. Thank you Lord, thank you. Amen." Her head was bowed, her eyes shut. While she prayed, Stan sat still, his eyes also closed. When he looked at her again, he knew why he never, ever, saw her cry. He stood up, kissed her forehead. "Love you, mom."

He went into his bedroom and called Leah on the phone. Leah's five year old son, Ray, answered the phone on the second ring, inquiring, "Who is it, Stan?" Leah was nearby, because Stan heard her voice in the background, "Ray!—I taught you how to answer the phone right. Now gimme that phone. Who is it, Stan? You lucky, boy!" Evidently Leah was in good spirits, for she got on the phone joking, "Stan, you want a kid? Really, I mean that, you want a five-year-old strong black boy with bright brown eyes and good teeth? You can have this one I got for little or nothing. Matter of fact, honey, I will pay you to take this one. Seriously."

"What's up, Lee, other than that son of yours just being a man. You know we men can anticipate things, like who's on the phone by the way it rings. Women's intuition, ha! Give me man's anticipation any day!" Stan found himself in good spirits, too. "So, how're you feeling, still tired?"

* * * * *

Leah and Ray had just gotten back from visiting Leah's sister in New York City for a week. They arrived in Buffalo yesterday. Stan picked them up at the Greyhound station. The Greyhound station in Buffalo was never empty. Yet, the majority of those in and around the place were not Greyhound's patrons, were not traveling, were not even there, as was Stan, to greet, or say goodbye to, loved ones. A sweeper was wearing a red Afro wig and dark blue shades. He sang as he swept, and nodded at every black person who passed. At one point, he paused to chat with a couple of geri-curled brothers who also worked in the place, but not for Greyhound. They pimped by. They sold their wares there—stolen watches, or cheaply-bought watches which looked like expensive stolen ones. There were a half-dozen "wandering young things," as Nancy called them, teenaged hookers, in tight designer jeans, t-shirts, and soiled tennis shoes. And there were those who apparently came to the station to eat and watch and sleep, escape loneliness by sitting in a busy place. They sat throughout the terminal, slouched or slumped or sitting up-right, sleeping or daydreaming, seemingly at peace, perhaps at peace. An old black man sitting in a pay, twenty-five cents tv seat across from Stan snored. His face reminded Stan of Elder Shaw, an evangelist at a church they used to attend. And there were other assorted individuals and groups. From the one religious group which, for that particular day, claimed the bus terminal's front sidewalk as its sanctuary and store; from the desperately religious to the religiously desperate, like the amputees who waited in front of the Greyhound as if it were the pool of Bethesda, as if there, where they were members of a multitude of "misfits," the miraculous would happen, a savior would see them and "trouble" the air, the sidewalk, the building, or their outstretched cups. And they would be healed. Made whole.

Stan felt a kinship with them as he sat waiting for his miracle, for the woman who wanted him to accept her as that. Leah was striking, tall, an inch or so beneath 6 ft. Mocha-colored, with vivid black hair which she wore pulled tightly back, and always a bit of make-up—black paint surrounding large brown eyes, long lashes which needed no help, full lips, sharp facial lines. She always wore dark clothing, even in summer. Old, well-fitted clothing. Natural fibers—cottons, silks, woolens, "I look best in conservative things. And they last." She was a chain smoker. Stan kidded that he knew her by the smell of her smoke. But the cigarettes lied about her. To him, they were a residue of Leah's past life, a life in which she tried to be, in her words, "a tough black bitch," meaning she ran away from home at fifteen because she was "pretty and older looking and a good entertainer," first following a traveling off-Broadway black musical which played Buffalo for a weekend and hooking up with the road manager who allowed himself to "be fooled into thinking I was nineteen, for some pussy." Eventually, she sang backup for Sister Salter, a girl group which once opened for the Isley Brothers. While on the road, she learned to "dance, choreograph, steal, sleep anywhere, and with anybody, man, woman or in between." For awhile, she "learned to love drugs," but then, when she found herself pregnant with Ray, she stopped. (She'd already had a miscarriage and an abortion—one every other year on the road.) She stopped not because of the baby, she offered, but really, "for myself. I wanted to know if I could see anything good through, you know?" So she dumped Ray's dad, left the road, and kept the kid. Now, she said she wanted to find God, Jesus, and her attraction to Stan was in part due to his church background.

They'd made love last night at Leah's apartment. It was small, always dark, never neat. Never neat, because Ray's toyland was the apartment's living room floor. However, he spent last night over his grandmother's, and the day was thus Leah's—to make mess, play music, and love her love alone. They made love on an enormous velour pillow on the living room floor. They'd done so before on it, and afterwards they would usually lounge, sprawl on the floor, naked and sweaty and tired and bold. But this time, Stan rose up, bringing Leah a red robe and wrapping a white towel around himself. He did this to take away, rather, remove from them, the aura which surrounded them after lovemaking, so that they could talk. Initially, about their first meeting, at the shoestore. She entered and ignored the other salesmen. The way she strutted by them, like a model on a runway, it was apparent that she wanted him to wait on her. He ignored her. Though he wanted the commission, he knew that if a woman came into the store to talk to him, she was safe. No one else would get her. And a sale was guaranteed. All he needed to do was keep looking good, and the customers came. Eventually, she slid up next to him, three display singles in her hand. "Wait on me?"

"Yeah, Lee the world's really messed up." You really can't describe it otherwise. Just plain messed the hell up." He laughed, leafing through the pages of a women's fashion magazine. He couldn't talk without doing something else simultaneously. Indoors, it'd be tinkering, doodling, sketching—outside, following passersby, the action of the street. He raised his eyes from the magazine to Leah's face, searching his for weaknesses. He lowered his eyes, back to the magazine. Wanted to close them—because the room was dark and all the bright pages were turned and, even though lovemaking was good, he didn't really love her. No, check that. He did love her, enough to be with her right now. Enough to know he'd love her for the rest of his life. And that he wanted to do good things for her and never hurt her, or Ray. But there was something missing.

"Lee, have you ever heard of a rational suicide?" He looked at her again and continued leafing through the magazine.

"That's crazy."

"Maybe it is crazy, Lee, but I saw a tv program on it a while ago, the notion that killing oneself can be a rational act of self-control. Why not take control of your life, including your death?"

She reached for the magazine which lay open in his lap and, looking at it, asked, "Why do you want to talk about death?" She tore a page out. Began to fold, make it smaller.

"Death is a part of life. I learned that as a boy in church. My father taught me well. And so have others. It's something you can't run from, so you might as well run to it, when you're ready."

"Can we please change the subject?"

"No. I look around and see people I used to go around with, and I think, `You ought to go ahead and end it before you get worse.' And I'm better off than most I see, but not really. A jock! A degree. A gig to go to. Rising professional—assistant manager. Hell, I'm 32 years old and fighting like hell. This is not what I planned to be doing, where I wanted to be after college." He rose and stood erect, with both his arms extended straight out in front. His palms were pointed up, at right angles. "Hell, Lee, never mind, don't even try to understand, 'cause you can't." Then, he dropped tro the floor catching himself with his hands and began pushing up rapidly, chanting loudly: "one—two—three—four—five—six—seven. . . ." At twenty, he stopped.

That was the closest he came to telling her, to telling anybody, about his cancer and his plan.

* * * * *

"Yeah, Stan, I'm tired. At first I was happy you called me back, but now I wish you hadn't."

"Thanks."

"It's like you work hard at being sad. You're what momma would call sorry. You ever heard that expression? Only with you, it's worse, 'cause you try to make everyday problems into big tragedies." She laughed. "All last week, while I was in New York, I thought about us, you. And I realized that you're lonely as hell. Even *when* we're together. But have you ever said anything like 'Leah, this is my problem?' Even last night, before we made love, I looked at you and saw sadness." Her voice was low. "Saw what momma would call sorriness, but worse, 'cause you seem to have to dramatize everything, put yourself on center stage, back on the track. Stan, your days as a star are over."

"Look, Lee, you want to spend our customary Sunday evening together?—if so, I'll come by after I finish working out."

"No. I don't know. Come if you want to. Bye, I've got to go see what Ray's getting into."

"Yeah."

* * * * *

As Richard knelt, he thought of his son. And his prayer was that his son try and understand. "Lord, help him to see my side. I need him to see my side."

The church was full. It was the period of prayer between Sunday School and the beginning of morning worship. By custom, worshippers came, knelt at the altar and prayed. Others sat in the pews. Richard wasn't the only one at the altar. But he struggled to his feet and left for home, because he knew that this was not the place for him this morning. Because he knew his son hurt. Because his son was his. Because his son would not admit that he was his. Because his son had tried, and Richard ignored him. His son no longer tried. He got up. And walked to the cloakroom, stepping over kneeling bodies, twisting around kneeling bodies.

He pushed through the door dividing the sanctuary and the cloakroom. Once there, he barely heard the moans, the hums, the groans of the supplicants. He was glad. He did not want to hear them this morning because they might tend to, no, they could not, they could not minimize, drown out, the cries of his son. Yet, he did not want to hear them this morning because he wanted nothing to do with them. He put on his coat. He went home.

Richard never returned home from church on Sundays this early so his return at 11 a.m. aroused his wife. Nancy had been dozing since Stan left her room. She was a light sleeper, something she'd practiced for years. She heard the door shut. At the first step, though, she knew: Richard. His tap for a step, sharp, quick—the beat of a snare drum. Up the stairs. Regular, rhythmic, a bit louder each. Stopping. At the head of the stairs, at her door. The first room one came to. When they "split," she insisted on it—either this room, or she'd leave. So she won. And in this, she maintained awareness, an ability to hear upstairs and down without opening her door. She rarely left this room when in the house. She didn't have to.

He knocked. . . . She disregarded. He came in, speaking first, as he did now.

"Nan, have you seen our son? I came home because I'm worried. You seen him?"

She said nothing. She knew why Richard came and why, rather than going to Stan's door, he knocked on hers and then entered her room. Which he seldom did any longer. Which he never did when she was there, going in only when it was empty to get things of his kept in it. She knew that he saw the same thing in their son as she. That he too was frightened by the sight. She saw it in Roy, after the war. The look of Job, she called it—"curse God and self and die." She wanted to know, though, how he detected it.

"Sit down."

He did and looked around her room. Their room. Their son was conceived here. During the early years, all their time spent here, their first fully furnished room. The warmest. Bright green, brown and brass. Nancy collected all in a matter of months. With little money, acquiring bit by bit. Much of it was used—some gifts, some bought cheaply, some pulled in from the street. She worked on each piece. Stripping, polishing, rubbing, refinishing. And feeling that what others could not use, did not know how to make good, she could, she did.

"You want to go in to him? Go on."

He said nothing.

"Go," she said. "You need to. He's troubled, Rich."

As in the church, he rose slowly, with a struggle. He fasted on Sundays 'till after morning service, and he felt famished. He desired to say, "Nan, why don't we go down, eat something and talk about our boy's troubles? Our troubles. Then we'll come up together to him." But he silently followed her directions, leaving the door ajar as he departed.

* * * * *

Stan retrieved the journal kept beneath his bed in a corner where two walls met. Written in daily, the last vestige of his college dream of being a writer. After college, an upcoming Olympic Trials was more important than anything, certainly than using his Communications degree. Then, there was his injury. So no Trials. While on the mend, he accepted a job as a sprints coach at a juco in Nebraska and met Sheila there. Following her graduation, they married, and he followed her to California, so she could write and produce. Then, he lost her. Who made him feel better after he lost track. (He never again ran competitively after his injury.) Lost her, after realizing he'd had enough of school and that working on a degree, even an MFA in writing from USC, wasn't for him. Lost her, after finding he didn't want to write for the latest Hollywood black sit-com or special; lost her, after it was apparent that any gig thrown his way was because he was Sheila Lattimore's husband. Lost her, after it became clear that not simply the style of writing, but the style of living he wanted would be better accomplished elsewhere. Lost her, after returning to North Platte to coach and their trying long-distance love, letters and cards, phone calls and flights; lost her, after seeing he couldn't coach his kids into becoming the runner he was. Lost her, after returning to L.A. and discovering that, despite love, they weren't a couple anymore. (He also learned, through one of her girlfriends, that Sheila lost their child due to a miscarriage. He was ignorant of Sheila's pregnancy.) Lost her, after she left L.A. to produce and direct something somewhere and he left too, for good. Lost her, and now he didn't know where she was, his world-class woman who reached a level in her pursuits that he ached to attain in his. (Lost her, their divorce was finalized through the mail.) Lost her, his Sheila, before eventually returning home, when he began to wonder if, somewhere along the way, he also lost himself.

And now, he couldn't find Sheila if his life depended on it. Perhaps it did. He still believed most of that stuff from church, about "calling and predestination and providence," but sometimes he wished he could erase the wedding, the marriage, the failure—or turn back at some point, and save it. Walk, like Jesus, on water; do *exactly* what Sheila needed from her man. Resurrect, revive, keep alive the Stan she fell in love with; and then use his power, like that of the Holy Ghost, to keep her, until the day of their redemption. But the last time there was an earthquake in Cali, in L.A., he wondered if his ex-wife was hurt or dead. She was raised by a grandmother who was now deceased, and there were no mutual friends, really, just his friends; and hers. (And hers wouldn't tell him her whereabouts; he'd asked.) His family never became hers. Their two lives never became one. A biblical mystery he believed, not simply because he was taught it, but because he lived it. There must be something binding two people together thicker than "love," lust or law. And he and Sheila never even had all of those. He recalled one of their nights together.

Content to live like strangers, Sheila sat on her side of the bed, doing her nails and reading a Hollywood mag. Barely speaking to each other, they hadn't touched, kissed, in months and, though they slept side by side in slumber, they used each other's back as a wall. Stan, reaching from his side of the bed across the invisible barrier, snatched the mag from her, with the words, "now you'll have to talk to me."

"Nigger, don't you ever snatch shit from me, you black son of bitch . . . ," she screamed, swinging on him, punching and scratching, while he sought to restraint her, mouthing, "I love you, baby," but trembling as he struggled to hold her.

"Stan, let me go. Take your motha fuckin' hands off me. I'll kill you. I hate you. I hate you. I hate you . . . ," she recited, straining to break his hold.

His restraining arms welcomed the missed touch of her soft, tender skin while his mind fought the venom of her words, "take your fuckin' hands off me. Don't you ever touch me. Leave me alone, let me go, now, Stan." His eyes, as he beheld them reflected in the bedroom mirror, were liars. Her pink laced nightie was ripped as she strained to escape; her eyes were bloodshot, as were his. With one hand, she was digging her fingernail file into his skin, drawing blood; with the other, she was flailing the air, as though reaching for an imaginary dock, a post, by which to pull away. She kicked him. But he wouldn't release her. And for her continual words, "motha fucka, let me go," he continually whispered, "no, Sheila, I love, you," til the blood she drew ran down his hand, to the floor . . . til he realized her will and words were stronger than his arms, and he couldn't hold her forever . . . .

They "patched" things up after that, in part due to her having to leave town for two weeks on a project. And when she returned, he was gone for a week, back to Buffalo to visit mom. Toward the end of their marriage, he was both anxious and afraid: anxious to do the right thing; and afraid that it would be the wrong. Evidently, he did the wrong. Evidently, he spoke a wrong word; remembered the wrong words; bought the wrong present. Or his clothes or his look weren't right for an occasion. But he never articulated any of this to Sheila. For him, their numerous arguments always contained an undercurrent of false arrogance—him wanting her to know that he was desirable, wanted by women besides her. Why? Perhaps because of his sentiment that he was competing with the world for her. Or perhaps because he knew, deep down, how good Sheila was, even though he played "I don't need you" games with her. Because he sometimes couldn't understand, and was even frightened by the rage of his beautiful black wife, that he wanted to shout at her, "Baby, I'm *not* your enemy. The world may be, but I'm not!"

But now, it was different. But now that he'd heard the words, "the cancer has come back, Stan," the world, the past, his times with Sheila took on new meaning. He wanted to be Lot's wife, to turn around, run back, fast as he could, to the cursed cities of his past, and undo, if he could, a curse or two. He wanted to change a word; a phone call, a turn run in a race, an ankle not wrapped tightly enough, so that there wouldn't have been an injury, a missing of the Olympic Trials. He wanted to trace his steps back to place in the path where Sheila dropped his hand, or he dropped hers.

He took out his daily journal but couldn't write anything. The blank white page seemed both vast and useless. He could draw on it; doodle, draw horsies or doggies or cars; tear it out and make a plane that would fly across the room or, if he opened the window, out into the world. But he couldn't use words; didn't see any use, so he turned back to an old, unfinished poem:

> *I've reached*
> *for big truths and tears,*
> *fought with them.*
> *Prayers were dreams*
> *of never-never land.*
> *I saw scars*
> *in my city's faces.*
> *I didn't see,*
> *troubled and concerned*
> *over many things . . . .*

That phrase, "troubled and concerned over many things" was a Sunday School/church line, from, where?—from something Jesus said to Martha or Mary—the Lazarus story. He smiled, realizing how he could never shake the old teachings, even subconsciously, especially subconsciously. He began to write: "What would you be doing if you were living your life exactly as you are supposed to? How would you live and move and act—every moment—if you did *exactly* what you felt you were supposed to be doing? Would you be in a different city, job, with a different person, or would you be *exactly, exactly,* where you are now? And what do you do with yourself if you ever, ever, stop feeling this way? Is it a sign, perhaps, that you just want to die?"

He stopped writing. He wanted to re-do everything wrong that he could. Help his parents either reconcile or leave each other or do something, anything, besides live in the limbo of a loveless, lustless, lifeless marriage. He wanted to cut, poison, or burn out all the cancers of his past, in his family, in his damned sorry-ass neighborhood. After seeing a tv program about an artist, a sculptor who committed a "rational suicide," he planned his death and funeral, just in case. He wouldn't allow the cancer to control his destiny. He would. Yet, he didn't really know if he could do any of it—effect changes in anybody's life or kill himself before the cancer. But he could try. Just in case, the funeral was planned, letters written, music selected. There was one piece of music essential to his funeral, "To Inscribe," by pianist Hassan Ib Ali, on an album he found in their basement. Rummaging, through damp old albums. Richard took them down after he returned to the church. As a child, Stan was forbidden to touch them. Kept in a service footlocker in his parent's bedroom, and brought out one at a time. A soft clean chamois used to dust them. And, every so often, some would be washed in kitchen dishwater and racked to dry. At those times, Stan ventured into the kitchen to view the shiny black platters as they dried in the dish rack. The album covers would be placed on the living room coffee table, and his father would lie on the sofa, reading album cover notes. Stan would go into the kitchen to view the albums drying, as the child rarely saw his father's albums "naked," as his mother called it. He would also walk through the living room, to see the album covers as they lay, opposite his father, spread out on the coffee table across from the sofa. Photos of black men playing horns; sepia sisters singin' the blues; full dark faces that seemed to float on the dark mahogany surface of the coffee table. . . . And now there was mildew on several covers—their bottom halves were worn away by wetness, portions of pictures and prose gone. Some of the pictures he remembered, like people he passed by on a busy street, people who called to him but who he was unable to answer at the time. He took the albums out of the boxes, one at a time, and read the cover notes, sitting in the basement in the evening with the lights off. He read in the dark, turning each so the little light in the basement hit part of the album cover, and he moved the cover in the light as he read.

"To Inscribe" was from Ali's only album. Only recording date. His first, last. Yet Ali was a legend among Philly jazz men. A man obsessed with, one who lived his life in, his music, his piano. Who cut only one album, as leader or sideman, who played with many, but recorded just once. A date, and the years, cut after cut, were pounded, sounded out, stroked, to the accompaniment of Max Roach on drums and Art Davis on bass. "To Inscribe," the last cut on the album, was Hassan solo. Playing the melody with one hand, improvising with the other; playing the lower register with one hand, the upper with the other; playing slow blues; playing rapidly, arpeggios—again and again, fingers to keys, over and over. The last cut on the album.

Stan retrieved the album, placed it on the turntable, turned on the stereo, put on the headphones. He lay back, his eyes closed. In Willard Park when he was six. Playing around in the park while his mother sat within eyesight on a bench, reading. On another bench, toward which the child's running took him, sat a grizzled, shabbily-dressed white man in grey and green, the color of the bench. Bending over, looking in the grass, the man seemed to grow out of the bench. Stan, at the side of the bench, joined him in looking down. Not moving, he spoke.

"Want to make some money, son? Find me a four-leaf clover, I'll give you a quarter."

Unsure the man owned a quarter to give, the child accepted. And searched. Flowers, weeds, and dandelions, countless blades of grass. Kneeling, sitting, crawling, on his hands and knees—green on them and on his seat. Like a deer, head turning—about, about. The man's search became his. He knew his mom would soon call him back. . . . A premature end to the search, when, predictably, she called him, told him it was time to go home and that if he wanted a quarter that bad all he needed to do was ask her. And, words said at a distance because his mom was ready and the man was still engrossed but seemingly stuck to the bench, moving nothing but his bowed head as he continued searching. It was strange he remembered it, abandoning the "quest," like a tear wiped away, unallowed to run its course, 'till time or air or distance wins.

The volume was turned up, so his father heard the cut as he entered. "Yeah, that Hassan. He was something. He could really play." He picked up the album cover from the stereo rack. "Yeah, this was one of my favorites. It's a collector's item. . . . The only album he cut. Played with a lot of folks, though . . . ." The music ceased. Stan didn't move. The turntable went around—its spin the loudest sound. Wondering how the bedroom door closed, Richard turned his head. Did he close it upon entering? Or was it shut due to a draft from the open window parallel to it, down the hall? Richard didn't know, but he felt the closed door's effect. His son hadn't moved since his entrance. He felt starved; he wished for the cut to play again. For it to give him something to say to his son.

"What do you want?" Stan referred to him as he nearly always did, in the second-person singular. It was as though he were an acquaintance whose name Stan could never recall.

"Nothing."

"Why aren't you at church?" Stan still hadn't moved, although it seemed to Rich that his boy was trying to stare through him.

"Son, this man's old. He has a son, so he couldn't stay at church this morning. He got up and left during prayer. When he saw his son early this morning he wanted to pull back the bedsheet. And see you"—Richard paused"—maybe to bless, maybe to grab to hug." He walked over to the room's window, facing it.

"Is that it?" Stan's headphones were off.

"Your mother," Richard continued, "is in her own world. The damned past. You are a showpiece. I was. A sign that she was alive and kicking after her first died. She was more than a sign to me—at first. She was my woman. My slender tree. Before we married, I used to pick her up, and we'd walk up and down streets. And she'd deal with her past all the while clutching onto me, her present, I thought. But I wasn't. I was compensation, repayment, something. And so are you." He turned from the window and looked at Stan.

There is a myth about the black man. That he is unfeeling. His much-discussed coolness. His minimal commitment. His main commitment to self—and slickness and silence. Cool. The father and the son. Neither spoke, moved. And the room revolved around them. The stereo. Turntable. A slight hum of the headphones. Richard could not close his eyes, like his son. Yet he could not look down at him or around the room. Wished himself blindfolded. Began to hum. "All night, all day, angels watching over me my Lord." Perhaps unconsciously, as second nature of a religious person, a Christian, one whose life revolves around the church, the gospel, the songs. Or, perhaps, in concert with the room's sounds. "All night, all day, angels watching over me."

Stan opened his eyes. Turned off the stereo. Stared at his father, and crossed the room, daring him to come closer, move, go for it. He took his jacket down from its hook on the wall and left.

* * * * *

The sky was golden with streaks of dark brown. A black cinder track with no one else on it. Which was why Stan came here Sunday evenings. At other times, it was monopolized by joggers, pale, slow people whose bodies hung like wet clothes as they ran. Pieces of cinder stuck in the soles of his running shoes as he walked. He dug in, pressed down hard, then began to run, launching forward, feeling the muscles in his calves tense, then stretch. Sprinting a turn, he leaned into it; gaining speed, . . . his lungs, arms, and legs synchronized, he dug into the black track, pierced through the evening air . . . .

The smell of spicy food and piss. A phone booth. A boarded-up, long gone-out-of-business gas station. A deserted corner. Sunday evening across from the University, few out. Most students in, studying to start the week. Stan left the stadium in his sweats. Was cold. Had two calls to make—to his mother, Leah. Dialing home. Holding the greasy black receiver close to, yet not touching, his ear or face. Letting it ring. Five, six, seven. Hanging it up, and again. No answer. Same with Leah. Deciding to go to BB's, to see if his mother was there. He didn't go there often; in fact, he only went in to pick her up. She didn't drive. Refused to learn, attributing this to her "three long years in New York City long ago" and to her desire to "be escorted as much as I can."

Seen through a glass door, the barroom shone. Brass and black wood. Stan stood in front of the door, looking in for a while before he entered. Soiled white sneakers on shining black marble floors. Walking lightly and slowly, like this familiar bar was a strange territory, a war zone. She wasn't here. The corner table where she always sat was encircled by men. He took a seat in the front, by a window to the street. A large, clear window, with stained glass panes and hanging plants blocking its center. It offered little view to the street.

Sunday nights were "oldies nights," blues, jazz, and early Motown tunes. Loud music, with lots of cymbal and bass in the sound. At intervals horns honked. A waitress/D.J. spun drinks and sounds to bunches of brothers sitting, standing around, shooting pool and the breeze. Working men, of the steel mills, auto and iron factories. And welfare men, laid off. Stocky, strong, black men who raised families, whose children were raising children. And long, lean, youngbloods, in to jive the old, play, pick up any of the young women who came in to pick up older men. Stan caught the eye of the bartender, Johnny, rose and walked to the edge of the bar. Johnny had bartended at BB's for years. It was rumored that he was part-owner, but Johnny never responded when asked about this. Stan felt that his mom knew, but she wouldn't tell him. Johnny's son, John Jr., Johnny Boy, who would have been Stan's age, died of sickle cell while they were high school juniors. Johnny marked his son's death by taking out a full page ad in *The Advocate*, the black community's newspaper. In bold letters across the top of the page were the words: JOHN JAMES "JOHNNY BOY" DAVIS, JR. Underneath this: FEBRUARY 5 1954-SEPTEMBER 29, 1971. A blow-up of Johnny Boy's high school senior photo, taken during his junior year, a montage effect—front facial portrait superimposed on a larger partial silhouette, followed. And beneath that, a brief letter: I AM INDEBTED TO THE COUNTLESS FRIENDS AND LOVED ONES OF BOTH MY SON AND MYSELF FOR THE CARE AND TOGETHERNESS EACH OF YOU HAS SHOWN, DURING THE DARKEST TIME OF MY LIFE WITH JOHNNY BOY'S PASSING. I THANK EACH AND EVERY ONE OF YOU, AND MAY THE FATHER BESTOW HIS BLESSING UPON YOU ALL. SORROWFULLY YOURS, "JOHNNY BOY'S" DAD, JOHN JAMES DAVIS, SR. And next to the closing, a small photo of himself, taken somewhere in the bar, in shades and applejack cap. After Stan received some notoriety due to his running, Johnny began fantasizing about how close Johnny Boy and Stan were as friends. They hadn't been. But Johnny held the delusion, which Stan never denied. As a result, two photos of Stan hung in the bar, surrounded by other photos, of black pros in basketball, football, baseball. And one of Martin and Malcolm together, smiling. One of the shots of Stan showed him breaking the tape at the NCAA's; the other, from the same meet, was of him and his relay teammates, smiling, hugging, and holding medals. Stan's solo shot was the most prominent, centered behind the bar, hung slightly higher than all the others, and his photo with the team was directly opposite it, above the front door. "Because Stan's local and he's my boy, too. And it's the next best to having Johnny Boy up there," were Johnny's words to Nancy when he surprise-unveiled them for her one Sunday. Their sons. That solidified their friendship.

"Stanford, what'll you have, son?"

"Orange juice."

"That all?" He grinned. "That all? You in training?" He placed his bar cloth and elbows on the bar.

"Yeah. Always."

"Well, you look in about as good a shape as back up there." Johnny jerked his thumb up toward the picture behind the bar.

"Better." Stan looked at it. "Better. But I need that juice."

"Sure son, no charge. How's your folks?" This last said as he walked to the refrigerator at the other end of the bar. "I suppose your mom'll come by tomorrow sometime." He returned with a tall glass of orange juice, a straw, and a napkin.

"Want some cashews?" Johnny went into his white apron's pocket, pulled out a bag.

"Thanks." Stan returned to his table. Sat. Staring at his glass and stirring ice and pulp with his straw. Although a section of the joint wasn't in his eyesight, he could see it through a large convex mirror above the bar. Thus, he watched a game of pool. Two young brothers stalked the table, cues up like spears, then down to shoot—blasting balls and bar talk and music. Through it the speeding, spinning balls played against the colors of the players. One dressed in rust three-piece suit, white shirt, top two buttons unfastened. And rust, leather and suede shoes. Brown brim. Gold on his fingers, round his wrist. Partner in rust, too. Rust sweat suit—with white stripes on the sides of the pants and at the jacket sleeve cuffs. Rust and brown suede tennis shoes. Brown baseball cap, the word "JAM" on it in white letters. Beyond the table, through the mirror, more talking, drinking, dancing people. And a young white woman. Staring. Back through the mirror at him. She looked white—now white, now not. He couldn't tell. She was very very light. She wasn't white. Her sloe eyes. Gave her away. Her full lips. And nose. Gave her away. And prominent cheekbones. And face. Her face gave her away through the mirror. A smirk on it, the kind street-smart little black kids give you when you give them less money than they asked for, than they begged for. It, the smirk, made him think her young. Know her black. . . . Not in the mirror now. He couldn't see her, but she was coming. He focused on the talk in the air: "Yeah, man. . . . Naw, you ain't gonna. . . . I can't afford nothing like that, but check this. Yeah, later. . . . Hey, blood, I ain't seen you in. . . ." Reappearing in a moment, now without the mirror, she looked like Leah. Just lighter. Toward him. Tall, long-limbed. Slender neck bent to a side. In a knee-length, black casual dress, wrapped by a belt of colors—green, red, black; and a big black sweater— maybe a man's sweater. The rest he couldn't see, tables in the way. Until she was next to him.

"You looking at me? Have a good look?" She paused. "Well, I've studied your picture for the last half hour. I don't know how long you were in here before I caught you in the mirror." She sat down.

"Hey."

"Hey—you come in *here* to drink orange juice?"

"Yeah, and for other reasons."

"Such as?" Her hands shifted an ashtray between them. She

picked up a matchbook which was in the ashtray, lit a match, tossed it in the tray. It went out en route. "How'd you feel when it was taken? That picture?"

"If you don't know it already, my name is Stan. Yours?"

"Puddin' Tang—ask me again." She smirked, scooted her chair, which had been adjacent his, around the table so that it was directly opposite his, so that it blocked him from the bar, virtually from the rest of the place.

"Serious."

"A while ago, I stopped worrying about the strength to do what I want to. And I want to talk to you. Serious." She struck another match; it flickered, died in her fingers. She tossed it at the ashtray, but missed the mark. "I've seen you around, Stan. Heard folks mention you. I'm curious."

"What brings you here?"

"My business. Not yours. OK?"

"For now." He looked at her glass. Smoke black. Wondered what was in it. She took small sips. He studied her face. Not that young, his age, or a bit younger. Around her eyes, brown pencil, black paint. Touched to lashes. Lips glistening red. And up to eyes. Green. He moved his hands over his hair, the coarse, oily texture felt good. "What do you want to talk about?"

"You. I want to talk about you."

His car followed hers. She drove carefully. Stopping at yellows. Signalling in plenty of time. Easy to follow. Soon they were in a section of Buffalo where few blacks lived. Large brick homes, separated from the street by expansive, well-manicured lawns. The lawns were still green. Half-moon driveways. She turned left into one such drive and stood halfway out of her car until his was also in the driveway. Other cars in the drive. An old Victorian home converted into studio apartments, six of them. She said she loved it, except that there were no other blacks here. Or around here. Just domestics. She loved them, too. There were mornings she jogged to see them. To talk, and, she put it, "to catch warm brown smiles." At first, the landlady thought she was white. "She didn't know what I was. She does now. More black folks came through this door when I was moving in. Like ants to a picnic. I threw a move-in party. Provided pizza, beer and herb. She stopped by and was standing in the drive, watching. She said something to an obviously black dude, who happened to be my brother. She laughed when he said so. I was at the top of the first flight, but I overheard them and hollered back, `Yes ma'am, he's mine, same momma, same daddy.' But she doesn't mind—I'm light enough that no one knows unless I tell them, and I pay on time."

When they reached her floor, the third, the top, music emanated from within her apartment. Entering, they found her turntable spinning, but not playing the disc on it. Sounds from a radio station came through the stereo speakers. "I must have left this on," she said, walking over to the turntable and putting its tone arm to its rest. "It's supposed to shut off automatically. I'm about a hundred yards from an FM station—there's a signal tower over there." She pointed at the only window in the apartment. "So, whenever the turntable or tape is on, I get easy listening music beneath my jazz." She smiled. "Please, have a seat, Stan." She tuned the stereo to an R&B station, turned up the amp, excused herself, and went to the bathroom at the apartment's rear. Stan sat to the right of the entry, directly opposite and staring at, the combination 'frig/range/sink/counter with cupboards above. Most of the apartment's furnishings lay on a shag rug: instead of a table, four black and scarlet oriental lap trays in a square, and four scarlet floor pillows, one behind each tray. Table lamps also rested on the rug, one on each side of her tray arrangement. Her bed, a mattress, resided just off the rug. Its red and black sheets were pulled tight. Her stereo was at the head of the bed. The television and two stereo speakers were directly across from the bed and adjacent to the cupboard.

Books were scattered over on that side of the room, piled up against walls, atop the tv and the counter.

She reentered, "You hungry?" Grabbing the refrigerator door, swinging it open and holding it, she proclaimed, "Look. See what's in here? Next time you come, I won't even do this." She smiled. Switching on the tv, but muting its sound, she explained, "I always do this when I'm listening to music. Especially if I'm alone . . . at times it even looks like the people on the screen are moving with the music." She laughed. "Almost. Usually they're white folks, can't move."

"You're crazy."

"About you." She sat down, resting against the frig.

"You don't even know me."

"I know you, Stan. I've studied you. Your picture. . . . Love at first."

He rose chuckling and walked to the window, "I came into BB's for my mom. She's usually there on Sunday nights. If you've been there some, you've seen her."

"Yeah, I've seen her. . . Sharp lady. Heard her talk, too. With Johnny and anybody else about you. And you. And you. . . . for three."

"For three?"

"Yes, dear, the perfect pair is three. Becomes three."

"Like those two fat fools around you at the bar, the ones I rescued you from, were really three. Right?"

"Stay on one subject, Stan. Anyway you're wrong. Those men were talking among themselves. And rescued? *I* came to *you*, Sir Galahad."

"Still, rescued."

"Ha—my black knight in shining sweats," she laughed, crawling on fours like a baby to the tv, turning up its sound, over that of the stereo. "I like this commercial." She rested about a foot from the screen.

"Why don't you turn down the stereo?"

"Do you smoke?—Nah, you don't." Crawling back to her mattress, she reached underneath, bringing out a small plastic bag.

"Not in years."

"Not ever. But you should—do you some good. I'm going to smoke just this joint and blow puffs of smoke your way. And you'll have a good contact. Hey, since you're over by the 'frig, would you reach up and grab down for me that book on top," she inhaled.

He lifted up to the counter/'frig top. "There're two books here. Which?"

The books were: A translation of *The Idiot,* by Dostoyevsky and, underneath it, *The Autobiography of Malcolm X.*

He reached underneath. "Here, you could use some Malcolm." He tossed the book at her, hitting her arm which held the joint.

Watching the book as it hit the rug, she brought the joint to her mouth and inhaled. She closed her eyes. "Hand me *The Idiot*, idiot," she smiled, pushing the book in front of her away with her foot.

He used his foot to nudge it back in her direction.

"You remind me of the main character in this—Prince Myshkin, the idiot. Check this." She read: "'Most illustrious Prince. Unvile in soul and spirit, but ask any man. But ask any man, any Blackard, even who'd he rather have dealings with, a Blackard like him or a most magnanimous man like you, open-hearted Prince? He replied that he'd rather deal with one of the most magnanimous men. And herein, sir, lies the triumph of virtue. Goodbye, my dear Prince. Gently does it. Gently does it. And together.'" She looked up. "Like you, Stan. Epileptic, Christian, gentle. The Prince, and you. All those. Or which ones, Stan? Epileptic? . . . Frenzied? . . . Or gentle, or together?. . . . Hmmm?"

"You know the answer."

"Because you're a jock? An ex-one at that?"

"I'm *ex*-nothing. Whatever I was, I still am." He got up. "Excuse me, I've got to use the rest room."

When he came back, she said, "Serious, Stan, you should check out Dostoyevsky . . . Serious Stan, you should. It's my second time reading this one. I took some courses down at U.B. Got into Continental writers—this guy, Tolstoy, Stendhal. My second time reading Malcolm's autobiography, too. I always read two books at once. For a change up, you know? You think I'm ill-mannered and forward, don't you? Well, I'm not. I like you." She got up halfway, on her knees. "I like you a lot. Your picture is something else. And I know you're still a jock. I've seen you running. You must wonder what I do. Hanging around bars. Picking up men. No, I don't." She inhaled on the joint. Was silent as a song started on the radio. A hard-blown sax was leading a combo. Weaving through a melody. Tightly stretching out sound, repeating, rehearsing each note, for the rest to follow. They did, giving more definition, but the sax dictated the sound. Now standing, she began to move. "You know, I'd love to shrink down and be inside the throat of that sax. Listen." The sax and trump were in harmony, blending layers of sound over the drums and bass. The piano picked its spots, syncopating between silences. "I'd love to be in that sax. Dancing inside its wet throat. Feeling power from whomever's blowing. It'd be slippery, but I'd hold my dance. Maybe even on my toes. Crazy, huh?" She danced directly over Stan. "You may wonder what I do for a living. I've modeled a bit. Downtown. Toronto once or twice. Thought about moving to New York, but no. That would be a trip in itself. Obviously I like to dress, sometimes. Some folks think I'm some kind of call girl because I go into BB's alone. But I'm not. Why be with a man for money or appearances or tradition? Right now, I'm a part- time receptionist."

"Facially, you remind of a sister I've dated, but that's where the resemblance ends. At first, I didn't really think you were a sister. I'm still not sure. I've read some of the books you mentioned."

"Good, now join me." She held out her hand. He did. Doing the dance he always did. Popping one finger, the left, to strengthen it, use it. Or clapping his hands hard, as in church. And sliding his feet—never lifting a foot entirely from the floor. His eyes riveted on his partner. Because she was audience and he actor. He stared, not so much at her face or body or her movements, as *through* them. And no matter what she did, he maintained his movements, rhythm, dance. And Claudia was good. When he asked her name as they left the bar, she slowly pronounced, "'Cloud-dia,' not 'Claw-dia'—I am not a cat, and I don't have claws. But I do love the sky and to get high, so remembering the clouds you'll remember how to say my name. . . ." A very good dancer. From her moves, he could tell she'd practiced dance. He kept time, but she played with it, playing the song with her body; however, unlike him, she didn't give him a single glance. He thought that perhaps she couldn't and continue her dance. Then, the cut ended. They stopped, as the sax cascaded into silence. . . . A ballad, Norman Conners' rendition of "Betcha by Golly Wow," with Phyllis Hyman on vocals.

"Now, you wanna dance with me?"—he touched her arm.

"That's the funny thing about the radio," as she stepped to him, they began. "You know they play the same old things. Top ten, top fifty, what's the diff'? You have no control, but it's predictable, so you wait. Every now, they slip one in on you. Like this one. They must have a different D.J. The regular one wouldn't play this—this one's a lot more laid back than the others." She paused. "'Laid back'; I hate that expression. And 'mellow', too. But what can you substitute for the word 'mellow?' 'Laid back?'—'cool?' I don't know, do you?" Their movement was minimal. Not too close, just a light brushing of thighs.

And neither knew who was leading. At one point, she sang softly, with the balladeer, and when the strings came in, she closed her eyes.

"A romantic, huh?"

"I love beauty," she replied. "Straight ahead of you. You're facing it. A little picture in a gold frame in the corner. Water and ships in the distance. And fog. It's a postcard I got from a friend. Sometimes I put myself on one of those ships. I'm doing it now, even though I don't see it. You do it too. Join me, on one of those ships. You'll pick the right one." She put her head on his shoulder. He focused on a sailboat in the picture, placing both of them on it. After the song ended, she left him standing in the middle of the room. She turned off the stereo, tv. "No need for these—we make our own sound, our own pictures." Closing the blinds, she put the chain on the door.

* * * * *

"When I was a child, thirteen, my sister Alma was 15. Alma became pregnant. My parents forced her to abort. Then, they made us both have our tubes tied, if you know what I mean. That's why I don't take anything. I take nothing . . . . Hey, listen, you've got to leave; I've got some changing to do. And some reading. And sleeping." She smiled. "So get up." She pinched his buttock. Seeing his surprised look, she grabbed the bedsheet, pulling it off of him and over her head. "As a matter-of-fact, think I'll sleep now," she said from beneath the sheet. "Shut the door tight when you leave."

When he finished dressing, Stan pulled the sheet from her face. "You don't have a phone."

"Yes I do. Down the stairs, down the street, on the corner, that's my phone. I put in my money, and that's my phone."

"You weren't asleep."

"I still am. I'm dreaming. So are you. . . . And in an emergency, I use the guy next door's. Nice guy. We play chess or tennis together sometimes. I think he had a crush on me. But I knocked that out. Threw my Malcolm on him. We started discussing books, Dostoyevsky, then I gave him Malcolm—the idiot." She smiled mischievously.

He kissed her smile. "Well, listen Claudia, what if I want to come over?"

"Just come."

CHAPTER
2
And I Saw

Stan didn't cry when he heard the news, when Maxine, Max's twin sister, called and told him that his running buddy drowned. He didn't cry as he struggled to understand how a strong swimmer, a native of the Islands who swam all his life, could drown. Instead, he asked when and where the services were so he could come. Instead, he tried to comfort Maxi with silence when she cried while telling him. He couldn't cry when she did, though he wanted to, perhaps because she was the subject of bantering between them, about how he was going to wine, dine, and wed her, beautiful black woman, a runner herself for a school in Texas, whom he hadn't met but whose pictures were the first ones Max showed him. Hers was a voice he heard over the phone previously, but never in tears; "never," the word Max would use to tell Stan when he could wed a Livingston. "We wouldn't have you, mon. You ain't bad enough. Yous bad, alright, for an American, but shit, you ain't black, yous a Canadian, from some damn cold-ass Buffalo."

He heard her tears the next day, on the drive to the airport. Her tears, and Max's laughter, laughter punctuated by profanity, seemed to mingle. No, not mingle, but vie for position in his mind, like on the track one stutter-steps, elbows, or strides out to get the inside lane. As the 747 took off, Max's laughter had it.

Maximillian Levant Livingston was his running buddy in college. Max was from the Bahamas, a dark little dude with bow legs and a barrel chest. His shiny black curly hair surrounded his face like a mane yet stopped just short of being a beard. They both ran the 400, and it took them four full years to discover who was fastest. They met and roomed together during freshman orientation and, subsequently, throughout several track seasons and school years. Their sophomore through senior years, after Stan won a full scholarship, they rented an apartment together. Actually, they roomed with another runner, Kojo Karikari, KK, a sprinter from Ghana. It was a two-bedroom apartment, but KK made a practice of returning to school late, so fall semesters he stayed with them because little else was available when he arrived.

They first raced the evening of orientation. After dinner in the dorm, they went walking, with Stan showing Max sights around campus that Max might've missed on his recruiting trip, or that the Coach surely wouldn't have shown him. They were recruited to run the same event, but Max arrived in Buffalo with the rep of being *bad*, the first top-level foreign runner the track program recruited or, as some said, "successfully recruited." Karikari signed on only after hearing that Max was coming. The boy's rep was that tough. Coach Bailey, the head coach, was quoted in the papers as saying, "the young man is good. He can put our program on the map all by himself." That first evening, as they talked and walked toward the track. Stan knew where they were headed, but he didn't know if Max knew.

"Hey mon, let's not go back to the fucking dorm," Max said in a deep West Indian accent that would make some, especially the white boys on the team, complain that they couldn't understand Max, and others, especially white girls, compliment him on his running, his 'fro, or his dress. "Yeah, mon, Stanley, shit, if my woman wasn't going to school in Toronto, mon, I wouldn't be here. And the damn coaches talking about how they gon build a program around me, like they gon have me run every damn race. They come down home talking 'bout opportunities up here. Coach Bailey, he gon tell me what a good school this one is. I tole him, `Coach, they all good schools—you Americans all say the same thing. Even you black ones.' I never seen a black mon blush, but Coach Bailey, he blush and start to say something when my daddy cut him off, saying, `that's right.' And mummy just sit there and nod her head. I could see right then that Bailey, he upset and disappointed, like he done blown it, cause he look like he want to leave right then. You know how folk start sitting up in they seat like they know they time is up? Well, mon, that's when I decided to come here. I say to myself, here's this brother trying, I say, trying, to be honest when we all know he can't be totally honest or I wouldn't the fuck leave Freeport. Ever, mon, for anything, I wouldn't leave atall." Max pulled out his wallet, and offered from it a young woman's picture, "Here's the real reason I left, anyway, Stanley. Allison, my womon, mon, she attends Ryerson. And this is the closest damn American school with a good program."

"She's alright, man," Stan said as he took from Max the snapshot of a smiling, pretty, honey bronze young woman in a black bikini. "Yeah, she's alright. Got any sisters?"

"No, mon, she's an only child. Spoiled, and I spoil her too." He took the photo from Stan, handed him another one. "That's my twin. Allison's my heart, mon, but Maxi's my soul."

"She's your twin, huh?" The photo was of them together, he in a track uniform, she in a dress which matched his uniform, arms around each others' waists. "So how come she's a fox and you're a dog?" Maxi was approximately the same height as her bro, with a full head of jet black hair. Her facial features, while resembling his, were more defined, yet softer.

They were outside the stadium now, and the track could be seen through its gates. "Hope I get to meet both of them some day, 'specially that fine sister of yours. You sure you're not lying about that? Her being your sis?. . . . Cause you're downright homely, man."

"The women don't think so, Stanley. And youse gonna find that out, motherfucker. You got a woman? Naw, you don't, but if by God's grace you do, watch out she don't fall for me. You wanna run some?" Max was unzipping his sweat jacket.

"Yeah, I'll run you, but after I whip you, you may wanna go on up to Toronto with your lady or back to the Islands. Cause this is my town, my stadium, my track, and I don't lose on it, dig, foreigner?"

"Yeah, I dig, you wanna get your ass ground into the track, so you'll have an excuse to quit before the season starts."

They were now on the infield, taking off their sweats, loosening up.

"And another thing, Maxwell, after I whip you tonight, you gonna call me by my right name?"

"And what is that?"

"Stanford or Stan, okay?"

"Sure." Max smiled. "A couple times around in a jog, and then we do it, okay, Stanley?" He held out his hand. Stan smacked it with his. "Deal."

That night laid the foundation for their friendship. Max won, pulling away during the first 100 meters and holding off Stan's surge over the last 100. They were close at the finish, though, maybe a couple of tenths of a second, if that. Stan knew that whatever time he ran was his best ever. He vowed then that before the end of the four years they'd be even closer at the finish. As he flopped next to Max on the grass infield and gazed up at the sky, he vowed to himself that they'd be closer by the school year's end and that, before it was done, their positions would invariably be reversed. He closed his eyes. "Next time, Brother Max, you're mine, hear me?"

"Yeah, I hear you, what you been doing, training every day or some shit? You pretty good, Stanley."

The name thing. If track solidified their bond, the names they gave each other that first year symbolized it. From that night forward, Stan called him "Brother Max," not always, but enough that it stuck. He called him "Brother Max" because, at first, it emphasized Stan's threat to "marry your sister, you ugly motherscrunchee." Later, it meant more, and might be said after a particularly tough practice when the coach was berating Max, "the imported star," for "not putting out like the rest of the team," or for resisting efforts to be entered in another event. Or it might be said after a victory or a record, by either of them. After awhile, it didn't matter; one breaking a record or winning was as good as the other. Almost. Their rivalry intensified during those four years. They competed constantly and over anything: other sports, cars they drove, seemingly out-of-their-league women. They shared: from cars to clothes to crises over racism or overdue assignments. Shared. So much so that the 1600 meter relay team, Max, Kojo, Stan, and one other runner, Alton, was labeled "the foreigners," not because they all were foreigners, but because Max was such a compelling, attractive, charismatic one. Black collegians from Africa and the Caribbean were constantly over to their apartment—to hang out with Max. He was the star, the brother the Islands who was defiantly proud of not being "like black Americans." He was always ready to party, with rum, reefer, and access to pretty women; to say nothing of his main squeeze, Allison, who resembled Dorothy Dandridge during her brief Hollywood heyday and possessed the British graces of a well-bred Bahamian young lady. The cat could do it all:

golf, play tennis or discuss world politics with the white boys;
party or run b-ball with the brothers from the street who were always wandering on campus for play; or discuss his schooling in
the British system and trips to London with white girls who, it was
apparent, wanted to find them a black boy(friend) just like him,
but couldn't. On their campus, Max was it. And his brethren from
the homeland and the Caribbean knew it. (Even the Jamaicans,
somebody observed.) Being labeled one of the foreigners, part of
"the brethren," Max's label, worked for Stan, and he was clandes-
tinely grateful for his friend's "expansion of your mind," another
of Max's phrases.

The name Max gave Stan was, simply, "Son." Its genesis was
after a home meet during the spring season of their freshman
year. During the past indoor season they finished one-two in virtually everything they competed in together, so Coach Bailey
decided to split them. Stan ran the 400, Max the 200, and they
competed on the relay team. Max also long and triple jumped.
They both took firsts in their solo events; Max a first and a second in his jumps. Their 4x400 meter relay also triumphed. Following the relay race, Nancy rushed from the stands, weaving,
pushing through the slow and stationary toward them. They
stood side by side, surrounded by reporters and other teammates. Their team won the meet easily, and they were discussing
their next contest, an away meet with tougher opponents. Ap-
proaching, Nancy heard them and, upon reaching the two,
hugged Max, saying that her "second son was so good that
when that team for next week reads about him, they might decide not to compete." Standing between her "two sons," she
put her arms around both of them, bringing them closer as she
embraced. She informed their amused teammates what they already knew, that her "two sons, my first one and my second son,
are going to rewrite the track record books for this school."
Thus, the team was given a new set of tags for Stan and Max:

"first and second son." The tags fit; went along with their being "foreigners." But Max's didn't last. He already had half a dozen nicknames, and they didn't need another one for him. In fact, he supplied them with new ones, such as proclaiming that his name was Maximillian Bonaparte Winston Churchill Toussaint L'Ouverture Levant Livingston and that, like Toussaint, he would kick white ass if he had to. But Stan needed a name. "Stan" didn't fit; it was too much the given name for them to use it on one of the stars they loved to deride. Stan's stuck. And was altered, for awhile, to "number one son." The team members liked that. It was a cliché they all knew, and fit well because it hinted at Stan's inscrutability. They didn't know if he loved or hated it. Wanted him to love it, just a bit, hoping that he would see their affection for him. But he didn't show them his feelings. Max, who always voiced his opinion on team matters such as this, was silent. Max, who long ago ceased calling him Stanley and never called him "number one son" because, humorous though it was, he felt it mocked a mother's love for her child, eventually offered his version. In the locker room before practice one day, he read aloud a news article on the two of them. Actually, it was on Stan's successes. The heading was "Native Son Challenges," and it related how Stan was competing on par with him, "the much-heralded Bahamian recruit." "Well, it's right," Max proclaimed, "Son, here, is one bad-ass runner." The name was given. And it stuck. Max let it rest so the team would pick it up. It was close to something they thought needled Stan. And it was shorter and faster for them to say, whether it was during a meet when they were cheering him to victory or during a locker room barb session, when his, or whoever's, verbal defeat was the goal. Max let it rest around them until he was sure that they wouldn't revert to the other. They didn't. But from that time on, he called him "Son."

"It means a lot of things, Son. That youse my ace, that I like your act, that I respect your bond with your mom. I don't know, bro, it fits, that's all. And if anybody on this damn team is gonna give you a name, it's gonna be me, somebody who can kick your ass in everything, got it?"

* * * * *

Max's older brother, Emmanuel, and Maxi met Stan at the airport. Alton Thomas, the fourth member of the relay team, arrived earlier that day. As casino manager for a hotel on Paradise Island, Emmanuel was putting them up in a complementary room. They came as Max's old friends, literally, his old running buddies, but also as ambassadors of his effect on America. "Youse some bad mothers—nobody else came from as far. You, Stan, came from Buffalo, and Alton, mon, he came from Seattle, Washington. You can't get farther than that and be in the States. When sis called him up, he started crying and said he'd be here if he had to sprint across the whole damn USA and swim the fucking rest. Sis said she knew he was a white boy, but Max never really made that distinction about him, just referred to yous by name and race, the distance of the races yous run, or ran in college. So, Maxi said, even though she knew he was white, she responded . . . "

". . . I responded by saying, bro, you know you're more than welcome, and if you come it'll be an honor to the family. You know, Max used to talk about how when yous went on track trips your nickname was 'four the hard way.' Said that's what you called yourself 'cause you were always jeopardizing your running in meets by partying, getting lost, and coming late. . . ."

* * * * *

Together, "four the hard way" invariably arrived late except, as Max would say, "at the finish line. There, mon, we always ahead." Except Stan, who never came late to anything—practice, meals, classes—unless he was with them. Stan looked forward to seeing Alton, his "alter ego." That they possessed similar surnames caused people to get them confused. And similar nicknames, Alton's was "Ton," also bestowed by Max. It fit. Ton. Big dude. Best 800 meter runner in the school's history. Ton, queer cat. One of them, but not black. A white boy, from North Platte, Nebraska. Who walked their walk, talked their talk, and could dance his ass off. Who bought them all "FOUR DE HARD WAY" t-shirts to wear over their uniforms. When he joined the team, it was whispered that he was a fag, and most of the team members kept their distance, joking behind his back, smirking to his face. However, watching him run the 400 one afternoon, Max uttered what Stan and he were silently thinking, "Cat can run his ass off. Runs like a brother." After saying this to Stan, Max yelled to Coach Bailey, "hey, mon, go get us three more white boys just like this one. Matter of fact, Bailey, take three of de ones we got now for trades." He shouted it loud enough that Alton, who was just finishing his sprint, heard. The team heard. Yeah, 'Ton was queer, big white dude with thunder thighs from years of dance training. During dance classes, he discovered his sexual preference and, during his junior year in high school, he also discovered that, as he told the trio, "I hated studying dance. In dance, it's about controlling energy, holding it in, rather than the exploding of it, the rapid all-out unleashing that track allows." While confessing this during one of their lockerroom raps, Alton also offered that, "explosiveness and vibrancy" were the reasons for his "attraction to blackness," black culture. He studied black dancers and runners, too, and modelled his styles in both "art forms" after blacks, not whites. "When I was in high school, there were many days when I wished I could be black. Now, I don't. I'm content with who I am. Most of the time," Alton added, grinning wryly, and knock-

ing on the wooden lockerroom bench. Queer, crazy, sincere
'Ton, the biggest sprinter on the team. Always into the weights,
6'1", 220, whom Max was always "trying" to get to go out for
football, "so we can manage, you, mon, big white boy like you,
who's fast and got those ballet moves. The NFL would love
you—the great white halfback hope, and you'd be bonafide.
We'd be rich motherfuckers." From his scrapbook, it seemed
'Ton might've made riches via dance, but he didn't want "to be
branded as a fairy in a stereotypical fairy profession." So he took
up track his senior year in high school and majored in Engineer-
ing at the university. And was *the* reason their 4x4OO relay won
at the Nationals Stan's senior year. 'Ton, was, as Max said, a
"bad-assed runner," but he was even "badder" in relays than in
his solo events. He held school records in the 800 and 1500
meters events, but those weren't his best distances. The 400
was. But it was Stan's primary race and one in which Max also
competed. Depending on if you considered Stan's competition
with Max a standoff, 'Ton was content with being second-, or
third-best on the team in this event. Queer. Because 'Ton's
times when they ran in the relay together were comparable, like
he ran harder in that damn relay than he did in his solo events.

Queer cat, the type who told you to your face, "I don't lie or
front on my friends, and anyone who does that to me, I don't
consider a friend." Queer boy, white, but not really, as he
"adopted" the black world as his, and fought hard, like any
brother, to defy the stereotypes of "his type." Queer 'Ton, and
queer all of them, hugging, dancing, four as one, after they took
the 4x400 at Nationals. They always decided among themselves
who ran in what position, switching from race to race, so no one
on the relay team could be labeled as *the* lead or *the* anchor.
Coach Bailey didn't care as long as they kept winning. This time,
Max led off, but stumbled out the blocks just a bit behind two
runners from West Coast colleges. Then, he didn't stride out

like he should've, and they fell further behind, three, four meters behind the top two. KK just seemed to be biding time, as if he were running into a non-existent headwind. The gap lengthened. For awhile, Stan was scared, watching 'Ton, waiting for the baton. They were five, six meters behind. But 'Ton ran third, and from the moment he grabbed the baton, it seemed that all their drive was his, like 'Ton simply said, "I'm tired of this mess," and put the pedal to the floor, like when one is driving up a hill and decides to get over the damn hill, now. Even if Stan closed his eyes while he waited, he would know what happened. The roar from the stands said 'Ton was doing it, sprinting out of his shorts, giving the bloods in the stadium loud questions, "Did you see that honkie kick ass? Pass those brothers like it was *his* track? You *sure* he a white boy?" Ton passed Stan the baton with three meters of track between their team and the others. The rest of the race was a breeze. Stan sped to the bedlam awaiting him, his bros with outstretched arms, clenched fists raised. Queer sight, their victory lap, three of them carrying the other a hundred meters or so, and then stopping so one of the carriers could be hoisted on the shoulders of the others. They gave Alton his turn last, taking him off the track on top, while that queer cat shed tears which Stan and the others held back. Later, they shared giddy laughter like only comrades can, about the race, the meet, and their times together. They stayed up the whole night, partying first with other teammates and friends, and then by themselves, until five, six a.m., over brews and sodas, chips and sounds, with large doses of Earth, Wind, and Fire, War, and Ton's favorite, Stevie Wonder. He must've spun the entire double-set album "Songs in the Key of Life," three, four times. This was their last race together because Max and Stan would graduate in June. From now on, the most they could ever be was training partners, competitors, and friends. At one point in the morning, 'Ton, or was it Max?, noted with sadness in his voice, "It's like we don't want to go to sleep, and wake up not being teammates anymore."

"Coming late"—in order, it was usually Ton, Son, Max, and then KK. "So maybe KK will show," Stan thought aloud; then, realizing the presence of Maxi and Manny, he became more deliberately silent. Maxi must have heard him, "It's a shame I couldn't reach Karikari, that nobody knows where he's at now."

"Alton, when I picked him up, said you was the one who kept everybody else in touch with what was happening with the other old teammates, corresponding and calling and that kinda shit," Emmanuel negotiated the car through the narrow streets of Nassau.

"Yeah, Max said you were like that deep down, loyal to the core," Maxi added. "And the writer of the group. And Alton was going to teach, KK to become a physician, and my brother . . ."

" . . . our bro, rich . . . wealthy. Eventually get that MBA and make big cash," added Maxi.

"This shouldn't be happening," thought Stan. He hadn't visited the Islands before. Max insisted that he come "anytime you feel like it," but invariably something intervened. Karikari visited once, for Max's big Olympics party, but that took place during the period of Stan's injury. "Max should be driving this sucker and calling me Son, telling me how great it is that I'm now in a black man's nation. I should be kidding him about these wrong-way dirt roads. . . . " Max bragged about the Junkanoo Festival and how eating conch contributed to his physical and sexual prowess. "I should be humming, 'Independence Bahamas. . . .'" The summer following their freshman year, Max stayed in Buffalo to make up classes, living in the dorm. He spent much time at Stan's that summer, fighting homesickness, wanting to go back so bad that he played to death, on Stan's stereo because he didn't have one, his records by Bahamian artists like Sparrow and his Independence Celebration album. "Independence Bahamas," a song from that album, became a joke and a symbol between them. It meant, "think homeward," so that if they were somewhere and Stan wanted Max to leave the scene, he hummed or sang it softly. Stan made leaps when using the song—sometimes it meant, "get lost so that I can be alone with her," but at other times it signalled "let's split," or "nothing's happening here," or "you're right, brother Max, the Bahamas would be better." On each of those times Max caught the message. He never missed.

* * * * *

Reverend Jacob Smythe wore a black clerical robe with a traditional collar and a black pillbox. He rose reciting a passage, Psalm 8:4. "What is mon, that thou art mindful of him?" Smythe read slowly, repeating the question thrice, "What-is mon?" He stood straight behind the pulpit, "What is mon?"— "What is mon?"—each time stressing the next word. He read slowly, stopping the third time, after "mon," and continuing only after each mourner had time to ponder, and answer, the question for themselves. "What is mon?" I'll tell you what he is. I'll tell you and answer two questions simultaneously." He boomed this last word, taking his loud time with it, as though each of the six syllables should fill not a second but a day. "Si-mul-ta-ne-ous-ly," he repeated the word, less loudly this time, but stretched out just as long, and then he stopped. Stood still. His black face and bald head glistened like obsidian. He leaned on the pulpit.

"Even a big mon seems little from a distance. I don't care how big, he seems little. You sit on park benches, like I do, and you watch a mon, and you see him small from a distance, till he get to you and your see his bigness, you appreciate his bigness. People look little from away, and they really are. They look like little figures that can't manage by themselves. They can't. The Word says that. And I say that's what we are. Little.

"No, beloved, Max didn't die because he couldn't swim. We all know he could. Could swim well, stroke with the best of them. I knew the boy from when his mummy first brought he and his siblings to Sunday School. No, even before that, to Vacation Bible. The boy couldn'na been more'n three. Sister Livingston brought the children here after the family moved to the neighborhood. And that boy was quite a runner then. He grew up to be a strong mon. An athlete. A track star here and in the States. Represented us in the Olympics. I myself saw him swim, watched him dive off rocks, and swim out where the boats go. Where the boats go, Beloved." Smythe paused, took off his glasses, raising his head to stare at them. "Maximillian could do a lot of things well with his body, and swim was one of them. He didn't drown because his time was up, Sister Inez." Saying this, he looked at Max's mom but pointed beyond her, to the pews packed tight with mourners, at the mouths which murmured that Max's death was fate, God's will, and that his time had come. "No—heaven no, his time hadn't come, and even if it had, that, Beloved, wasn't really the reason Max is gone." Earlier, as he pointed at the crowd Smythe descended the steps and strode slowly toward them. Now, he ascended the steps to the pulpit, but he didn't turn his back; rather, he slowly backed up the steps, the bottom front of his robe sweeping them as he ascended.

"Max died because, as big and beautiful as he was, he was little. Up close, that boy was grand. Young, smart, athletic, with a good future." He stepped back from the pulpit. "A future that tragically drowned in the bay. Really, Max was little and flawed. No different than any mon. Or womon, Sister Inez," he said, smiling at Max's mom, "or womon."

What is mon? Mon is as a college friend of mine used to tell me about my outlook on some things. This fellow was radical; I was not. He would say that my mind was *too* little. Maybe. But I know, 'cause The Book tells me so, that mon is too little. *Too* little. You, me, us all. I'm not here to praise Max—he was a good guy; I tole him so when I saw him. He wasn't a perfect guy. I tole him that, too. I'm here to tell you to remember his life as a grand one. It was; he made his mummy happy and his family and friends proud. That is a fact, not a judgment. We can't judge his life and put him in heaven or hell. That's God's province. We're too little for that. We can only, recall his life and laugh or cry and thank Jesus for him. We're too little to do much else. . . ."

Smythe might have said more, Stan didn't remember. He did remember, though, how he, Ton, and the other pallbearers wheeled the shiny, jet casket behind Smythe, the family, and a marching band. He remembered the band—three trumpets, a sax, two bongos, a conga, and a snare—the small, steadily marching band. These young men, Max's homeboys, did not march as in a parade, show-stepping, like the Buffalo Brown Cadets. Their steps were not fast, as though they were in a rush. Neither was their walk deliberately slow; nor did it seem a stomp calculated, as with juveniles in a frat or a gang, to call attention to themselves, to shout their petty pride or cause. No, this was the march of strong young men whose brer died. They didn't shout their sorrow; they strode it. Like the walk of a prideful man, rich or poor, who knows who he is and from whence he has come, they stepped aright. Their instruments swayed; they did not. The onlookers who lined the streets of Nassau as they marched from church to grave nodded and bobbed heads, rocked to the music. They, the band, did not. They—from Emmanuel in front on sax, to Decky and Rod behind him on trumpets, to the others—played with their heads held high, their eyes straight ahead, focusing on the narrow way before them. The dirt road on which they walked seemed, to Stan, like the aisle a choir marches up. One knows, in such short marches, one's immediate goal, to get to the choir loft. One also knows that, once there, the march is finished but not over. One has a job to do once one is there, and that job is the reason one has marched. Watching this tiny band of Bahamians, Stan knew well why he never heard the term "choirboys" applied to the males in a black church choir, regardless of the choir's composition of the sexes, regardless of the ages of the males in it. There are simply some things in the black community, worldwide, Stan sensed as he watched the band, that "boys" are not allowed to do. These were *men* playing for their dead, most dread, bro.

They arrived at the gravesite and, at first, played a dirgeful rendition of "Amazing Grace." Then, it was "Nearer My God to Thee." They played together and took turns soloing. Emmanuel's sax growled, scraped, bowed, and soared. Then, while they played "Coming Home," a quartet of homegirls sang the song. Smythe read The Word—"ashes to ashes," and all that went with it. After him the band took over again, with "Nearer My God to Me" and others. They played for, Stan guessed, twenty, thirty minutes. The more they played, trumpet blaring, sax wailing, the more tears came. It seemed they were calling, for the tears to descend, or the dead to rise, or despair to, like the tears, run its course and disappear. It was different from any funeral he ever attended. It possibly wasn't the most tragic. He'd attended funerals where the deceased died younger, where the death was more dramatic, and where, in life, the dead was less loved; no, it wasn't the most tragic. But it was the saddest. It reminded him of how he or Max sought solace during women woes, playing a sad love song over and over, to try to recapture, through depth of remembrance, the depth of love once felt. Or a hard-ass day of training, running sprints with Max or Ton or KK, over and over, the same distance, the same speed, the same cinder and sky and body that wants to quit yet simultaneously wants to never stop. And the white tent covering the mourners couldn't shade them all from the sun. So there they were, bunched around the plot like little children watching a schoolyard spat. No one seemed to move, as if the fight wasn't finished, and they were awaiting another shove, the next blow. . . .

Maxi began reciting her elegy for Max. Stan didn't hear its title, didn't know if it was titled. Throughout the funeral, Maxi clutched Manny's and her mother's hands and cried profusely, her petite body heaving like a tree bowing to the wind. Tears streamed from behind black sunglasses, down her cheeks, while she faced the black and gold casket. But before speaking, she must've wiped them away. Her face was unstreaked. Its dark brown shone like beautiful, polished wood. She held her head high, her voice fluttering at first, and spoke firmly:

Twins: two so like
each other - myself
and my brother,
a nativity of two,
Me and you.

Our baby love
beginnings
were framed
in photos
of parental pride.

Our adolescent love
was felt
through spites and fights
which grew as we
to shared foes and goals.

Our big love
grew bad
like you
and me, your Maxi,
as you named me.
Twins: two beginning,
growing, loving together;
born to be so,
and that's why I know
you're alive, Max, in me.

Stan kept a copy of her poem. He requested one later that afternoon at the Livingstons' house as black-clothed mourners
milled about, sitting four on a sofa, two in a chair, standing side
by side against a wall, or partially blocking a doorway. They
weren't really mourners anymore, but they were. Now, eating
chicken or fish and rice and rolls and yams, drinking coffee, it
was certain that they had passed from one stage to the next. The
men and boys opened top buttons, loosened or unknotted dark
ties. The women walked in their stockingfeet. They *had* all left
the grave, yet they seemed to be waiting. In linen and cotton
and silk, they seemed, like Lazarus, to be wrapped in grave
clothes, waiting to be unwound. Sitting, standing, moving,
smiling, they seemed to wait for a Savior, one who would loose
them, whose words would be, "let them go."

* * * * *

He rolled over on his bed. It had been his all his life, all his
memory. At eight, after he outgrew his current bed, Nancy took
him downtown to Victor's, a furniture store. He imagined that
the store was connected with RCA Victor. It wasn't, but the

false image added to his awe of it. The store was huge, Buffalo's biggest. There was furniture up to the front door, with big leather couches outside the store's offices. He sank into the soft, worn burgundy leather, enjoying its soft, supple feel in his hands, its slipperiness against his dungarees. Liked looking out on the field of furniture, watching salespeople scurry across. After she returned from one of the offices where she opened her account, they rode the elevator upstairs. She decided that it was the bed for him. Her Stanford could grow in it, and when he married, it was big enough for both. It was a bed for life. He'd never need another, as it was full sized, and the wood was solid oak. The salesman knocked on it and invited them to do so. He looked at his mom, was it alright to do so? "Honey, you'll grow up in this bed. And your daddy and I won't ever have to buy you another. If you want to, you can hit it a couple of times, knock it good. It's yours. There's not another one like it on this floor. You can bounce on it, baby. We're gonna get the mattress, too." Perhaps the bed was "big enough for both" but, after their marriage, Sheila never accompanied him home. Funny, how he thought about Sheila at the darnedest times—a song might do it, or movie, or even this bed. They made love in this bed once during their first months, his bringing home to mom "the only woman I've ever wanted to marry." It was passionate, unhurried, unrushed. Their three years of married life seemed rushed—from the start to the finish, never seeming like it would last. There was never the funky, leave-all-you-got, spontaneous, lovemaking he needed. She was a good friend with whom he lived. Some people were made to just be friends, and they'll break your heart if you try for more. Sheila was the aggressor in their lovemaking that one time in this bed, this room. And then, never again. In bed, she never initiated a damn thing but sleep. Eventually, he became used to it. Made do with it, with her, with himself. He made love to her while she slept, undressing, kissing, touching, opening and entering his sleeping wife, until she awakened with him inside. Funny, though she complained about it, she never made him stop. Made love with himself while she slept. She joked about it, calling him "too horny Harry," but he tried to reason with her that he wouldn't have to if they made love more than once a month. "Nothin' happenin' in that bed but sleep" was how he characterized his marriage to Max. "Ice maiden," was what he called her, and she loved it, felt she needed to be that way. Toward the end, he'd taken to calling her "non-fucking ice maiden. Big shot ice baby," screaming it at her, just to get a response from the woman he loved but knew he was losing. Baby. He didn't know she was carrying theirs. She left quickly. Not one for words, she said, "If I leave you, I'll go quickly, Stan. I'll go gently. One day, I'll just disappear. Life's too short to agonize over a marriage." No. No. No, in thunder. Life's too long to live with regret. From his father's church, repent, yes. But regret, no, not anything. But how could he not regret Sheila? How could he regret not returning to this bed, with his bride, or even shipping the damned thing across the country, from Buffalo to L.A., to try to remake the magic?

It was time to get up, date with Dia today. He recorded a tape for her, containing some of his favorite songs on it—by Marvin, Minnie Riperton, Donnie Hathaway, and the O-Jays: "The Dia Tape." A sunny October Saturday, after a hell of a week, finally, the weekend. He had the day off from work. Down there to get his money. They were paid out of the cash register. After picking it up, he would spend some of it on her. He wasn't going to conduct business with it, pay bills. And now dressed, he descended, past his father's closed door—actually, not completely closed— open about an inch, and he could see him on the floor beside the bed in prayer. Wanted to kick the door open. He passed his mom's door, and she was resting on her bed, but her head was up and her eyes were open. She looked at him, said nothing. He turned, went down the stairs, quickly. The first flight, seven steps. The last five leapt down, then the second flight, five more stairs, and landing made him stumble. He grasped the railing. Wood painted white. He helped him to do it six years ago. He paused as he remembered. Kitchen doorway on the right, to the outside on the left. White doorway, same job and time as the other. And afterward he told Stan, "good job."

When Dia opened her door she pointed with her free hand to a black graphic equalizer on the floor in the middle of the entrance. If not for her pointing at it, he would have tripped over it. "It's yours," she said, walking to the bathroom.

He bent down to examine it, "What'd you do, get this hot, or steal it yourself?"

She answered his question upon reentering. "Neither, honey," she smiled, tapping her mouth with her index finger. "I charged it and went up to my limit. But it was on sale, and I liked the way it looked. You know what it's for, right? It gives you a lot more selectivity and control. And Stan," she pointed at him, "it's good to look at—caught my eye."

He smiled. "Thanks."

When they got to his car he rested it on the rear seat. It was black metal with red lights. He kept the passenger's door open for her to enter. "Do you have the owner's manual and warranty?"

"No, honey, I threw them away with the box. Of course I do. I'll give them to you. Let's go," she shut the car door. "I took it out of the box 'cause I hate giving things wrapped or covered. I like giving *naked* presents, so the impact is immediate, one way or the other. Either the recipient loves or hates it right away, and I know which one. When I was a kid, I used to get more excited about the wrapping on presents, and then after awhile, I found out that what's inside doesn't usually live up to the wrapping.

Wrapping and boxes are p.r., so when I give anything I give without any of that outside b.s."

Driving, he clicked on the stereo and popped in Dia's tape. "This is yours, hon." Minnie Riperton, with the sound of a sparrow in the background, sang, "Lovin' You." The car cruised in rhythm to Minnie's sweet song, and they held hands, Dia softly singing along with her tape, while Stan tapped out the tune on the dash. They drove to an area on the outskirts of downtown where, Dia said, "College kids, blacks, and foreigners lived." They both loved this area. Had each loved it, in fact, before they knew and loved each other. It was close to where she lived but, as she said, "the mix is much better here. It's closer to reality." By "reality," she meant black folks. Neighborhoods where, among other things, she knew, "I can get some starch to eat. I was one of those little black babies who grew to adolescence eating Argo Gloss starch straight out of the box and welfare peanut butter and pasteurized cheese. Even though we weren't ever on welfare."

According to Dia, they were both "pack rats," collecting and keeping "things with little present utility, but you never know." They both loved to browse through old book and record stores, even Goodwill stores. This area was home to all of the above, as well as a "greasy spoon" restaurant she hipped him to that served the best omelets and freshly squeezed o.j. Their final stop was going to be Fields, a little black-owned store not far from BB's, which sold starch. They shopped, arm in arm, humming Minnie's tune and the Isleys' "Living for the Love of You." The crisp Buffalo breeze, coming off the lake made them hold each other more tightly. Or was that because of their ongoing duet? She found him a Coltrane record "you, no, *we*, have to have": Trane's *Ballads*. At Goodwill she bought two books: a first edition of Ann Petry's *The Street* and an anthology of the English

Romantic poets. Breakfast was great, as she shared his waffles, and he her mushroom and cheese omelet. The pot of herbal tea, and Donny Hathaway's "Take a Love Song," went together perfectly. As they drove to Fields, she talked animatedly, but he said nothing, enjoying the Indian summer sun shining through the windshield, beckoning them to follow, making him wish he could drive them away to where this day would be forever. He squeezed her hand securely to Marvin Gaye's "If I Should Die Tonight." Listening, he thought of "four de hard way," of running and winning, or not winning, but doing something that you know, you know, you've been put here to do. She looked up from her book; for a moment, she ceased humming. "What?" her face seemed to say. Then, it was obvious she knew, and she returned to her reading and humming. He wanted to say how special this day was for him, how he could just watch her eat and experience a high. Wanted to confess about his illness and fight and flight home and fears and damned scared-to-death-of-death nights. How he needed to go to the doctor, to check on the disease. But he was feeling fine, and wasn't the idea to beat it? He sped faster, concentrating on the traffic, on his movements; his right hand shifting gears—the knob feeling slick, the result of his polishing it. Clinch, shift, jerk, foot down. And a quick stop at a stop sign. Thumbing through the poetry anthology, she murmured something about how Marvin's song reminded her of Keats' poem, "When I Have Fears." It was like she could read his mind. He said he recalled it from either high school or college. Now, almost there, accelerating from the stop and shifting gears again, he decided to take the expressway, even though the distance was short. Using the access lane to hit it, and merging with the traffic already on. Once the last song on the tape played, she ejected it and began singing the theme from "High Noon"—"Do Not Forsake Me O My Darling"—one of her favorite movies. His, too. Rolling down the window for a moment, not thinking that the breeze might chill her. And then rolling it up again. Coming off the expressway by maneuvering through several cars and over two lanes. And opening the air vents as he came to a stop sign. Familiar because he daily stopped at it. No, never really stopped, not anymore, instead coasting to and through it, then making the left turn while thinking of other things. Like how she was saying she knew starch wasn't good for her but that he used to eat it when he was young because "we all did." Thinking, then, about finding a good parking space near the store, so they wouldn't have far to walk. So he could let her go in by herself if he decided to. He couldn't decide. And parallel-parking the car and asking her how near the curb it was. And getting out with her, buying starch, and heading back to her place. On the way, she took out the starch, began eating it. She didn't offer any, but concentrated on *The Street*. She'd purchased everything she wanted. She was glad. He was.

His life reached a regularity. Daily, there was Dia, running, lifting, and work. It was a frightening regularity. He recalled a line from a movie once, "don't trust happiness." He didn't. Losing Sheila taught him that. Max's death. The disease taught him that.

* * * * *

He opened the shoe store's door, went to the rear, sat down. Looked around. Before him, the sales floor gleamed pink and gold. Well-worn, wall-to-wall pink carpet, bordered in gold. Display tables the color of eggshells. Once, perhaps, to someone's eyes, a pretty store. (If no shoes cluttered the displays and no people the aisles.) But it was not now. It reminded him of a time on Uncle Marv's farm near Schenectady, when he chased chickens and was chased in return by one. The chicken coop was golden as the sun shone; outside it, the soil was pinkish brown. Pink, the color of his mother's blouse as she puffed Newports while talking with her brother. He pushed his four-year-old way through the gate and into the pen. Pursued—cautiously—two forward steps, then still, or one backward. Continually looking back toward gate and mother. And then, the pursuer, pursued, chased by a big chicken, so that he crashed through the gate and scurried to the skirt of his mom. Who hadn't seen but who, he thought, watched and supported the venture, but who now was scolding him. This event: perhaps his first realization that this parent—in some ways, in his mind even then, the only parent—couldn't protect totally, wasn't perfect.

He rose and ventured back to the office, actually, the desk he shared with Steve, the manager, to get his cup. A picture of three little blond kids backed by a Scandinavian-looking young woman identified Steve's side of the desk. It was a mess—utensils to stretch shoes, rubber heel guards, several cans of black polish, pens, and stacks of papers hid the oak of the desk. You could tell it was made of oak by Stan's side. A white porcelain cup, and three neat piles of paper were the subjects of staff jokes about their two managers. As one now-gone part-timer said, "I never knew niggers could be so neat." Overhearing what wasn't meant for him, Stan grabbed him, instinctively, like he passed a baton, but with both hands, and glared, reluctant to retaliate, as he should, with his fists. After some wrangling, and threats by Stan to go above Steve's head, the part-timer was fired. (But Max, he knew, would have offed the M.F., no pause, no questions, no regrets.) And Stan maintained his side even better. "When the Regional VP's come, Steve, you should put Bonnie and the kids' picture on Stan's side and sit his cup on top of your mountain of mess," was the joke of Chris, the cashier, before visits by company execs. Others said things like, "look at the managers' desk, you wanna see who really runs this place." Or, "you want the outgoing inventory, look in pile number one on Stannie's side, you want the staff schedules and duties, check his pile number two; you want the buyers' projections for next season, they're in his third pile; you want anything else, start fishin' in the mess."

He took this job upon returning home because he thought it'd be easy. With his degree, teaching, and coaching experience, he was overqualified, but that merely made it easy to obtain. Besides, he sold shoes once for this company before—the summer after freshman year, when he helped "babysit" homesick Max. However, he hated the job, and it wasn't easy, because he had to be here and put up with the other salespersons and the customers. He took this job because he needed the cash, and the insurance coverage was good. Unlike in PA, he didn't tell anyone on the job. People treated you differently when they were informed you had cancer, no matter how healthy you looked. They assumed you couldn't work or shouldn't work. They began waiting for you to die. Meeting Leah was the best thing that happened on this job. Now, however, that also complicated his life. Maybe his life wasn't all that complicated. You get cancer, you die.

Usually, by nine a.m. he heated water and made coffee. Then he tidied up the store and stockroom and waited for the others to arrive. Today was no different. He went back into the stockroom to make coffee, the job of the first person in. On alternate Mondays, as assistant manager, he came in first. Between he and Steve, whomever hadn't worked the previous weekend came in first the following Monday. Monday was a long day, open 'till nine. Many Mondays he would drive home at 5:00 p.m. and come back at 6:30 in time for the evening rush. The rest of the

day he worked the floor, taking his tea and snacks between customers, breaking only for the men's room. He was glad that
Mondays weren't busy unless it was near a holiday or the first or
last of a month. He sat on top of a stack of cartons, stared at the
coffee percolator, listened to the boil of the water inside. Visualized bubbles forming, disappearing, waves swishing. "Like
people, damned people. Gets hot, we jump." He tripped on a
shoe which was in the middle of the stockroom aisle. It was an
older style, from a shipment of a season or two ago. Its mate was
definitely not on display. The shoe was a white fabric, square-
toed dress pump, with a slight platform sole and a short fat heel.
It sold, as one of the salesmen, Jimmy, said, to "the unaccompa-
nied youngsters and the indigents." Young black girls and poor
whites of any age liked the style. Stan hated it. While it was still
in vogue and selling, he used a single of it as a hammer when
putting up a sales incentive poster. They kept a singles wall,
which was a receptacle for unmated shoes. Rather than shelve
the shoe there, he picked it up and threw it at an old poster of a
woman wearing their shoes, carrying one of their purses. The
shoe and purse shone, bright brown patent, while the rest of the
woman, except a brown pillbox, was drab gray. She almost
blended into the stockroom wall. If one just glanced, all one saw
were the shoes, purse, hat, seemingly attached to no one. Her
face was obliterated long ago by salesmen who, angry at customers for trying on but not buying or at other salesmen for stealing
buyers, threw shoes, balls, darts. She was their "f" lady—frustra-
tion, fun, you name it. He aimed neither at her face nor her mid-
section, the usual target of touches, object of jokes, but at the
point where her heart would be. Shouted, "You're not the vic-
tim you make yourself out to be. You're really a grey, heartless,
stonehearted bitch. And I don't feel sorry for you anymore." He
thought of Sheila. The shoe bounced off her bosom back at

him; he drop-kicked it toward her. On Mondays he usually ran the vacuum on the sales floor, but not today. Instead, he walked over the carpet, surveyed it, and picked up any large pieces of lint or paper he saw. Kneeled down and picked them up. Walked behind the customers' chairs and picked up papers. At one spot, on his knees to look in a corner. "Forget the creases," he thought. "It's 8:55, few more minutes, and the guys will be coming in." It was his job to open the safe and put in the cash register drawer bundles of ones and fives and rolls of coins underneath the drawer. Larger bills would come in as customers did. Besides, half of their customers would charge. He checked to make sure there were enough charge receipts.

A few customers came. As assistant manager, he was on salary plus commission, but he gave away to Tom what would have been his best customer of the day. Many of the women who traveled from Toronto to shop Buffalo's stores dressed exquisitely. This one did—she was tall and pale and looked like money. The red leather coat draped over her shoulders said money. Said she need not shop at their store. At first, she stood outside for about five, taking in the displays. Tom was in the front of the store, blocking the door. He did this to get the "up," so that customers, like her, would walk dead into him. When she came in, though, she brushed by him, ignored Jimmy, and went straight to where Stan was seated, inquiring, "wait on me?" Tom looked over his glasses, muttering, "must be one of Stannie's call customers."

She wasn't. Stan never saw her before and initially thought to sell her the damned displays if he could. He wanted to be with Claudia. Wanted, for a second, to grab this white woman by the waist and hold her. Tight. And make her wonder what he would do next. But he rose and escorted her to the front, to Tom's section, telling her on the way, "I'm on break."

* * * * *

Tacked on Dia's door, when he arrived, was a note—"Next door at Pete's, C-4, playing 'gammon." To his knock, she shouted, "Come on in, honey." When he entered, she said, "I thought it was you." She winked, smiled, and blew him a kiss. "I knew it was." She and Pete sat in the middle of the floor, on opposite sides of a backgammon board.

She sprang from a lotus position and kissed him. "Oops, I'll do you too, Pete." She kissed them identically, cupping their faces in her hands, bringing her lips to theirs fully and holding for a second or two. "Stan, Pete; Pete, Stan." Pete came over to shake Stan's hand, his right extended with thumb separated, to do the "soul shake." Stan didn't offer his hand in this fashion, and when Pete reached out, Stan held back until Pete brought his thumb back to his hand so they could shake in the standard manner. Pete looked Jewish, with a large face, curly brown hair, beard. He was big, with no definition to his sloppy body. Although the apartment was not warm, all he wore was a white t-shirt, damp with sweat, and dingy yellow gym shorts. "Must be trying to look sexy or some foolishness," thought Stan. Claudia and Pete shared a box of Argo Gloss starch. It was between them next to the playing board, and from time to time as the game progressed they would dip into the box and break off a piece of starch. A can of soda was next to the starch, and in it were two straws. There needn't have been, though, as Claudia alone was drinking. Pete won, and after the game, Stan started to leave. "Ready?" He looked down at Dia.

"Not really; you interrupted the tournament." She questioned Pete, "You gonna give me a chance to get revenge?"

"Now?"

"No, when we get married—of course now."

"You've got company."

"Stan's my man. He's not company."

"Let's go," Stan grasped her arm, to help pull her up.

"You go."

"Dia, I'm kinda tired, anyway," Pete reasoned.

"Pete, you're not tired. If Stan wasn't here, you'd play with me all night."

"Dia, I'm going," Stan released her arm, turning away.

"Pete?" she stared at him, cocking her head like a puppy studying a human.

"I really am kinda tired."

"Okay Pete, you win, but not the tournament. That continues," she said, taking one last sip from the straw and rising slowly, elegantly.

Once outside, she walked in front of Stan, facing him, "Don't pull that big, bad, black motherfucker shit with me."

"Don't curse me."

"You may intimidate white people and some women with your size and your stare, Stan, Son, whatever the hell you call yourself, but not me. Not me." She hesitated opening the door to her apartment, although her key was in the lock.

"I didn't like the way you were playing with me and that fat slob."

"That *fat slob* is a friend of mine. You're my man. Like you said, I was just playing, so what's the problem?"

"You won't open the door," he replied, turning the key in the lock, opening the door.

* * * * *

He kept his eyes closed when they made love. Couldn't remember if he had the first time, but from the second on, he knew. Didn't know why he did, except that it was like descending in a plane. Above the clouds, knowing there's an earth below with busy highways and speeding cars. And houses and rows of farmland. One cannot see them but knows they're there. Breaking through the clouds toward earth, one sees all as tiny. But soon, rows of tiny houses, lines of little cars, become Colonials and Chevys. Soon, descending, the unknown becomes the familiar. . . . Above her, his arms extended, she seemed distant. With his eyes closed, the same. But then, soon, it was like touching down in a plane. He opened his eyes. She embraced him, held him. And they talked.

She took him through her scrapbook. Page by page. First, it seemed all blacks and whites. Baby pictures. Fat-baby pictures. "My dad snapped a ton of these. And movies—we must have been the first black family in the world to have a sound movie camera. My folks would invite the neighborhood over, to talk and pose and later to view themselves. And me, the whole damn neighborhood grew up seeing home movies of me. Naked, with dirty clothes on, it didn't matter, if my dad took a movie of me that way, he'd show it. You know what my folks almost named me? Cleopatra—no shit, Stan. . . . Hey, hon, look at this pic of Cleon and me."

"Saturday nights, Dia, they're wild. My mom, she's always out. That chick will *not* stay home on a Saturday night. And she'll say it. Tell you why, too. . . . "

"My sister had to abort. She was sixteen. She said it felt like her insides were being scraped out. Know how to use a spatula to scrape a bowl? Well, like that, she said, only it felt cold and hard. It didn't hurt, but she could feel it. Do you know what it's like having your tubes tied? Afterward, right afterward, it felt like nothing happened, but I knew that knot was there. And after that, shit, Stan, I went out and tried to become the whore that the knot allowed me to be." She smoothed her arched eyebrows, "Truth is, after that, I did give away my virginity; I'm not going to go into it. I used to think I did it because I was robbed, raped of a precious part of my womanhood. I was. But now I know I also did it because the knot gave me license. For awhile, that bothered me, Stan, you know, like I was a slut who just needed the opportunity to become one. But truth is, honey, sometimes back then I could feel that damn knot. Knot of safety. I just wish I was given the option. Of even being able to abort. . . ."

"Dia, there've been times when I've sat in an airport or a hotel lobby and seen all those prosperous looking businessmen, with grey or navy suits who look like the million dollar business deal. They look like they've got money banked, invested, and no real bills, real comfortable in their whiteness. But then I look at them at times, and I say no—hell no—I wouldn't change the socks on my feet for theirs. I want nothing that they have, their money or positions or whatever. It's intriguing to try to figure out if some of them are as well off as they look. There've been times when I've felt like my proper place was in front of those m.f.'s with an outstretched hand holding a cup. . . . Max used to talk, on road trips, about what would happen if we were stuck in an elevator with some of those dudes. You know, what would happen if we were on a bus or plane that was stranded or an elevator that stopped, and there wasn't enough food or women for all of us. 'Who would'da won just now, Son? Us—or them?' One time we were on an elevator in an old hotel on 42nd Street in New York. We were running in an invitational meet in the Garden. Just us were there from the school, not even Coach. There were two stewardesses, a sister and a white chick, about five white businessmen-looking dudes, and us in this elevator. We got on last. Those white mother scrunchees weren't going to hold the elevator for us. They saw us shouting and running toward it, loaded down with our bags, and they just stared. One of the chicks stopped the damned elevator for us. So when we got on, I just said, `thanks,' cause I wasn't sure who to thank. Max reaches across the elevator, pushing against a couple of the men, and presses button ten. It seems we're all going up, to floors eight and up, so it's gonna be a ride. The stewardesses are to the side where we are, away from the buttons. The white cats are on the other side. The women are fine. One of the chicks makes a remark about close quarters. One of the white cats responds by saying something like, `honey, you can come up to my quarters and be close anytime.' It was the sister, cause Max goes wild. He just starts saying stuff to me, like, `Shit, Son, what if this damned elevator stopped here, what would happen? Who the fuck would get the women?' That sucker got quiet. One of the chicks said something like `hey, what do you mean?'—but Max kept on going: `I mean, sister, who in here would be bad enough that you would consider him as a damn possibility? I mean bro and me here, we're men of the body and mind, and we know would win in any encounter. Kick ass and get the women, if there's one to be gotten.' Those white guys didn't say a damn thing."

"Was Max your hero?"

"No. I don't have any heroes. I guess I looked up to Max. But . . . my father. He's my model. . . . Whatever he has done or would do, I do the opposite."

He shifted to his side, and stared at her. Lying on her stomach, she was still naked. Having tossed the sheet and blanket off her back, Dia was covered from the thighs down. Unlike him, she could sleep without covers. He needed something over his eyes, a pillow, a sheet, something to "close out the world."

"Stan, what's your problem?" She returned his stare with her own. "Look at the ceiling, the window, whatever, but take your eyes off me, okay?"

". . . I want to talk to you about something."

"Talk."

"Wait." He rose and put in "The Dia tape," fast-forwarding it to a certain selection. "Stay, babe, please stay, don't go away!"

Marvin Gaye moaned pleaded, begged from the speakers. Stan ached to tell her he was in love with her, but she knew that, didn't she? Wanted to propose something, marriage, engagement, something closer than what they were now. "So, what do we do with each other?"

"What we're doing now is fine." She was dozing.

He wanted to say, "no, it isn't, I want more," but didn't. "I think we're good for one another."

"We are, now. Isn't that enough? Strange things happen when people get closer, when they become a couple." Her eyes were closed and she smiled like she always did before entering dreamland.

"No, it isn't." He didn't want her to sleep, yet. He wanted to tell her about his plans, but she was sleepy. And he couldn't predict her response. Marvin pleaded, "Please stay, please, don't go away." The song made him think of Max—during one trip home, he borrowed Stan's red knit cap like Marvin wore on the *Let's Get it On* album. That, and Stan's black suede jacket. "I can kinda understand the jacket, maybe, but what're you going to do with the cap in Nassau?" "Wear the motherfucker, mon. Wear it like me boy Gaye," was Max's slyly grinning answer.

"Well, boy, you've got a problem then, 'cause I like things just the way they are," she said, pulling him from his thoughts.

"I'm going to listen to the rest of the tape with the headphones. I'm not sleepy." He kissed her cheek. "I'm gonna turn out the light, okay?"

"Fine."

He sat in the dark listening repeatedly to one song on the tape, the Isley Brothers' "Let Me Down Easy." Each day with her was better. It scared him. What could he say to her? He wasn't sure, and there was no one he could ask, except his journal. He took off the headphones and asked, "So, where should I put us, put you?"

"Nowhere, Stan. I put myself where I want to."

In the dark, his eyes closed, he caressed her smooth, soft back with both hands, like it was a magic lamp, thinking, hoping, that if he rubbed right, *his* answer would come. "You know why I returned home, right?"

"Yeah, your folks."

"And me."

"Of course you. What're you trying to say, Stan? I'm sleepy."

She revived in him emotions he hadn't felt in years. But he was afraid of taking her back, to the diagnosis; to when the biopsy "came back positive," in the words of his first doctor in Harrisburg, Dr. Parker. To his initial thoughts about suicide. To Dr. Goldstein, who encouraged him that, "we can beat this thing." What did he call it, "fractionated dose chemotherapy. The benefits of chemo, Stan, but less discomfort." It worked, for awhile. But the disease returned and he did, to the treatments, until he stopped taking his medicine, or rather, the doctor's medicine, and made up his own. Because he was sick and tired of the treatments. Tired of the thought of more radiation or even having to take that medicine for the rest of his life. He wanted to take her back to when he began to study the disease, in the middle of months of treatments, after the disease returned, like a burglar to the scene of a successful robbery, to rob again. And all he could do was put new locks on the doors and sit with his gun and wait. Well, he loaded his gun, but he wasn't just sitting and waiting. And he wasn't just calling the cops, the doctors, and hoping they could solve the case, catch the crook or whatever. No, he was going to beat this thing or die, but not die of despair, and not die because the disease won. He was going to win either way. He wished he could tell her, show her how his journal chronicled the story, the strange story, of where he was now. But he wasn't alone. In spite of the way in which he was fighting the thief, he wasn't alone; the journal was much more than just his. Though he kept one most of his life, since the onset of the disease, it included a "cancer section," a record of the lives, and deaths, of cancer patients. He clipped every newspaper or magazine article regarding a cancer patient, whether they were still fighting the disease or had succumbed. Like that in a black woman's magazine regarding a sister from Brooklyn who had a mastectomy, was doing chemo, and wrote, "I still feel like dancing." Or the white politician who fought colon cancer into remission and remarked, "this is just how it was meant to happen, all of it." Or Zack, the rich little white boy, son of one of the most powerful men in Harrisburg, whose battle against the disease was the subject of several news stories. When Zack died at age 13, Stan stared at the news story, read it, disbelieving, and read it again, while Otis Redding wailed in the background about "The Dock of the Bay." In an interview weeks before his death, Zack termed himself, "the luckiest kid alive," as he reflected on a loving family and friends. Stan remembered these people, their stories, not just because he collected them, but because they served as his "great cloud of witnesses." He wished he could've met them. Heroes. He could show her heroes. At times, these people were the only reasons he'd held on, taken his treatment. Sometimes, he dialogued with them, penning questions to them in his journal. He pulled back the covers from the rest of her body and began stroking her slumbering body, slowly, from the ankles up. As his hands moved upward, he whispered his witness, "I have cancer."

CHAPTER

3

Under the Sun

When two are together as lovers, spouses, or the closest of friends, folk think of them as a pair; when one's name is said, the other's is brought to mind. With Nancy, it was always, "Stan and me." During his boyhood, it was, "I'm taking Stan"—to the zoo, the circus, or shopping, "to get us some clothes." When he grew, matured and started dating, he also started driving, and that simply meant she wasn't reliant on Rich to drive her anymore. It became, "Stan is taking me."

"Mama's boy"—through the years, she smiled, inside and out, when she heard that label applied to her Stan. He was, but it didn't mean what some said. It described the closeness of their bond; that she was his favorite in the world; that she could depend on him like he on her. *Mama's boy* also meant that she was the *boy's Mama*, that she had entre' into his heart like he into hers. She never thought in terms of "love" when it came to Stan and anyone else in the universe, not even Rich; definitely not Rich. Comparatively, no one but she loved him. She sometimes wondered how God could love her son more than she. And she never regarded any of the women he was with and her Stan as a couple. To do so would mean deleting "Stan and me" from her vocabulary. Would mean that her *Mama's boy* was somebody else's boy first. Sheila, she disliked from the beginning—the girl acted siddity, smug, as though *she* were doing Stan a favor. And the way they got married—just doing it, without telling anyone or inviting a soul. However, they didn't last long enough for it to do anything but break his heart. And yes, she felt angry and sad and helpless because losing this girl broke his heart as much as losing track and Max's death. But secretly, she was glad.

Until recently, there was no one in his life he seemed serious about. Obviously, his experience with Sheila soured him about love the way losing Max and the strength in his leg made him skeptical about life. With Leah, whom he dated since returning home, Nancy wasn't forced to delete her name; he was still *her boy* first. Stan wasn't going to be this girl's. "Leah and Stan" was comfortable, because Leah really cared for him. A man needed a good woman, a woman who cared. So, even after the months, she very much liked the thought of Leah being her son's girl. *She* was still his woman. But when Stan began to seem different for several weeks; when he left early without saying anything on a Saturday; and when he neglected to call or come nights in a row, she began to wonder.

She sat at her kitchen table. It was against a wall, between two windows. Three sides of it were accessible, and chairs were placed at them. Each of the chairs belonged to a member of the house. Rich and Stan sat by the windows. She took the middle seat, that opposite the wall between the two windows that her men stared out of during their meals. Rich to her left; Stan, her right. But they didn't eat together anymore. Several layers of shellac glazed this thick-topped table. She shellacked it. Her place was marked by cigarette burns. When she came home feeling good, perhaps just a little drunk, she entered through the side door to the kitchen, and she sat and listened to the radio on the table. She might talk on the phone, although she seldom called people anymore, and an ash might drop, or a cigarette dip out of her hand not holding the receiver. Usually, she caught or snuffed out the cigarettes before they touched and burned the table. When she was that drunk, which was seldom, Stan would sit with her if he was home. Sit, silent, and extinguish cigarettes or catch ashes and butts; and listen. Listen. Nod his head or reply "yes" to something she said that needed it. She'd needed that boy's "yes" so many times, times she recalled so vividly that they seemed to be shelved, like library books in their sections. Her section, his. Though he never admitted it, she knew that there were times when her son needed her "yes." Times when he sat at this table, stared at the window, and just thought, or studied. Throughout college, it served as his desk, and even though he used pads, there were marks in the wood from his writing, which testified to how hard he bore down—through paper and pad and into the wood grain. Sometimes she tried to read the marks in the table, and she wondered which classes they represented, what assignments, even the names of the profs. Tonight, she was doing just that, deciphering his marks in the table. She never complained about his scarring it, because of what he accomplished. Her family's first college graduate. She was proud of him. So proud. So glad she was able to help him succeed in school by providing this place to work. It was a good place to work. Its white walls were painted annually. "Your kitchen should not only be the cleanest room in your house, but the prettiest, too," she told him while they were cleaning it. "You make sure when you get married that your lady can clean a kitchen, and that you can, too. I know you can because I'm teaching you everyday, but I want you to remember that it's not just women's work. It's family work. All this talk about `family rooms,' when your kitchen is your real family room. It's where you go as a family first thing in the morning, to get nourishment, say grace, and give nourishment and grace to one another before splitting up for the day. Your grandma used to say, 'you never know when you get up from the table and leave to go out into the world, if the world is going to let you or your loved one return.'"

Tonight, as she listened to the radio, she periodically turned the dial. At one end of the dial, the University station played jazz: Miles, Monk, Sarah V., Charlie P., all "the old masters," as she called them. From there, she might have to turn to the opposite end, to the local R&B station, to "catch a classic," before they reverted back to "jump up music." When that happened, she turned to her three standbys. Two played easy-listening music, music which "did" for a song or two, 'til she could find something with more soul. The last was a gospel format station that, during these hours, featured performers like Mahalia and played songs like "Amazing Grace." Such songs were touchstones, compelling her to hum, sing, cry, for the old times; and, after listening to them awhile, she might move the dial down and hope to get a slow Trane tune where no words were needed; or up, and hope that a classic by Sam (Cooke) or 'Retha or Otis (Redding) was playing. They sang psalms, like the Biblical David, songs about "lying and loving, failing and falling." They sang spirituals. Tonight, she needed them, the spirituals. Now, a woman was wailing, while a choir accompanied, shouting about "goin' through." It was almost 2:15. She snuffed out her smoke. Reaching across the table, she turned off the sound. Went upstairs and changed. She came down. She left.

She usually wore a scarf wrapped tightly around her head when her hair hadn't been done in awhile. Her scarves were of three solid colors: red, blue, or black. She wore one now as she walked the streets looking for her son. Black scarf this morning, and black woolen jacket. She didn't think she was going to find him. Didn't think he was there. But she must walk. Wasn't sure why, but she must. Her black leather slacks were too tight. They were the first things she grabbed. Her black woolen turtleneck was folded neatly underneath them on the rocker in her room. It, and the slacks, which she wore only when she was going "out," made her perspire. It wasn't rainy or cloudy, just humid. She carried an umbrella. It was 2:30 a.m., and Stan still wasn't home. That didn't concern her, and wasn't the reason she was out. He was grown, had lived all over the country. Furthermore, he grew up in these streets, knew them well, and anywhere he went in them, he was known. And Stanford could handle himself. Yet, in some ways, she knew, and she quickened her pace as she thought this, her son was still a boy. Not a boy who needed protection any more, like the time she searched for the housing project toughs who ransacked their neighborhood, stealing bikes, and jumped on Stan, taking his. She attempted to track him down, the ring leader, pulling nine-year old Stan along with her, back into the Talbert Mall projects, looking for, as she called him, "the slapper." She was determined to stand there and let them fight, one-on-one, and "whoever won could have the damned bike." But the boy was nowhere to be found. Nancy imagined that all mothers who are attentive to their children know ways in which, no matter how old, they are yet just that, children. Who need them. But Stan was changed. No, not changed in that he didn't love her. He did. And showed it in the same ways as always, hugs and "I love yous." The difference was that he seemed more given to something than ever before. More than to his bodybuilding or track or music or Sheila, or her. . . .

She was there. Knocking on the door lightly, as it was early morning. No answer. There was no bell to buzz. After what seemed like four, five minutes, she knocked again, this time less lightly. This time, she rapped on the door's tiny window with the point of her umbrella. Soon, light came. Leah and her boy answered the door. She didn't unhook the chain that held it, but

Nancy could see enough of the boy to know that he, half-asleep, was resting his head on his momma's waist.

"Is Stan here, Leah? If he's asleep, don't wake him. . . ."

". . . hi, Mrs. Thompson. No, he's not here. I don't know where Stan is."

"May I come in, Leah?"

Leah unhooked the chain that held the door. "Come on in. Sit down . . . please. I'll be back. I've got to get Ray back to bed. He's like me, a light sleeper." This last said as she lifted the big boy who slumped over her right shoulder like Santa's sack.

Watching the girl take her son to bed, Nancy knew at least one reason for Stan's attraction to her. She was quite pretty, with a fine shape, and there was an air about her that let you know she wanted to be trusted. Could be trusted.

"Your place is nice," she said as Leah sat down. "I should know it . . . but I forgot your son's name. You know mine's. . . ." She smiled, straightened herself on the sofa.

"I don't . . . Ray . . . his name's Ray." Leah flipped the edge of her robe to cover her knees. "Mrs. Thompson, I care a lot for your son. But I can't tell you anything about Stan that you don't already know. Matter of fact, I haven't seen him in six days."

"Leah, I'm going to go now. Thank you for letting me wake you." She smiled, held out her hand, preparing to leave. Leave, not because Leah couldn't answer her questions; not even because the girl looked tired and so sleepy; but because Leah was worried. Looked, talked, with worry in her voice. It was, Nancy sensed, over Stan. And she didn't want to burden Leah more with her own worries about the man they both loved.

"Mrs. Thompson, you don't have to leave yet." She covered the older woman's offered hand with both of hers. "Once I'm up like this, it's hard for me to sleep. Let's go in the kitchen; I'll make some cocoa."

"Coffee."

"Coming up."

Nancy followed Leah into the kitchen and began to talk.

"When he was a baby, he would cry, mmh. He came early, at seven months, and a big little sucker for his age. 6 pounds, 6 ounces, 19 inches long. They let me take him home two days after they released me. Stan didn't seem to cry that much in the hospital. But when we brought him home, he would scream like he saw God. Louder than I could shout. Sometimes, Leah, he would cry nonstop for hours—and there was nothing I could do to stop it. I tried giving him the breast, holding him, humming to him. That little sugar seemed to be saying that there was something he didn't like, I didn't know what, but it hurt that I couldn't prevent the tears and didn't even know why they came . . . those little baby tears hurt me more than anything since, . . . about anything. They got me ready, though. Anything he did later which hurt me, I kinda could handle it. To hear Stan talk about me, I can't handle things when it comes to him, but I can. . . .

". . . Yes, Leah," Nancy continued, "that boy and I have a strange bond, like when he hurts, I hurt, and vice-versa. You know when he was running, I don't care where, here, California, wherever, and he pulled something, I felt it? Like his junior year, he was running at the Drake Relays, and he pulled a hamstring, do you know my hamstring, on the same side leg, started hurting that day? When Stan called me that night to tell me, I already knew. One other time before that was real strange. I fell on ice and hurt my hip real bad—bruised it, you know? And when I fell that night, walking back from BB's, Stan was in high school, playing basketball in some tournament, and he got a hip-pointer that night. Somebody set a pick on him and knocked him down. . . . When my baby hurts, I hurt, and vice-versa. . . ."

"I'll tell you why Stan likes music so much. Jazz. When he was an infant his daddy carried him in front of the phonograph and played Dizzy, Miles, Bird, all the old masters. He held that little sugar's ear near the speaker, course it wasn't up too loud. And Rich talked to him, saying things like, `Listen to the way he phrases,' or, `check out that bass.' It seemed like Stanford understood—one month, two months old, that's when Rich started doing that, and that little sugar'd perk up. Rich fed and burped in rhythm with the music. I used to call him `Daddy's be-bop baby.' . . . `Daddy's bebop baby.' I don't remember when that ended, when Rich stopped doing that. . . .

". . . There was a time when Rich and I went out on the town together, the show, parties, plays. We did it up. There was even a time when we attended church together. Even on Saturdays, 'cause he was Youth Pastor for awhile, you know, and there were singings, special programs. . . . But now Rich, when he's not at church, he'll just as soon sit in his room and listen to the radio while he reads, or does nothing. He's not Youth Pastor anymore. Some Saturdays, it's like he just wants to get clearly one station that says "Jesus is Lord." Even if I'm downstairs, I can hear him. He'll tune and retune that radio. It's like he's at war with the static, or like he thinks the static is at war with God's Word, and he's got to get it just right. Half of the time, he doesn't even like the white folks he listens to. Just listening 'cause they talk about Jesus. Then they say something that pisses him off, and he switches to another. Between them pissing him off and the stations signing off, his options get narrowed. He switches I don't know how many times some nights. Starts at FM, until the two local stations sign off, then gets an FM out of Toronto, until the wee hours of the morning catch him tuning in Bible Belt stations, Ohio, Indiana, on AM. It's funny, girl, 'cause some nights we'll end up on the same station, and I'll be able to hear his so well I can turn mine off. We'll end up listening to the same thing, though goodness knows we didn't start off the same.

"When Stan was still very small, I would go to the bus terminal and sit. Sometimes I get like my momma; I just want to be in a busy place, surrounded by people. Momma used to say, `you hardly ever saw Jesus alone, doing nothing. He was with God in prayer or with people, giving them His energy, His love, and getting something, energy maybe, from them too.' Sometimes I go to one of the shopping malls. They're cleaner than downtown. Have more eating places but, you know, they seem like outposts."

"Outposts?"

"Sitting at the edge of the city, Leah, it seems like they're frontier forts designed to separate the settlers and the Indians. And you know who's the Indians," she chuckled, "so I don't go to them that often. I go to BB's. . . ."

They talked into the light of the morning. By then, it was the give and give of "sisters"; the hours and words and drink formed a bond. Nancy leading, Leah following—Leah interjecting bits as Nancy set her words like one might a dinner table. A bond, until sighs and smiles were joined by hand gestures and touches. A dinner table, plate by plate, silver in its place. Gestures, touches were done with ease. They felt, by the morning's light, that something more than a man bound them. . . .

"Leah, I've got to go now." Nancy snuffed out a smoke, ground it into the ashtray until in bent, broke in two.

"Yes ma'am, and I need to go to bed myself, before Ray bounces on top of me in a couple hours. Did Stan do that when he was little? Wake you up at the darndest times?" She drank the last drop of coffee in her cup.

"I told you six hours ago," Nancy rose smiling, knowing it hadn't been that many hours, "to not call me `ma'am' or Mrs. Thompson or any of that. My parents named me Nancy, and anything other than that is usually unnecessary. Of course Stan woke me up at crazy times. That's one of the things kids do well—keep you awake and then wake you up early when you're asleep. You know that. I know you don't drink, so I won't invite you to BB's, but let's go to the show together some time. You know I don't drive, so you can be chauffeur, and good company, too. Now let me be going before I fall asleep in your kitchen." She opened her arms to embrace Leah, who was also standing.

"Nancy, I want to fall asleep—quick, fast, and in a hurry. I don't care where." Leah rubbed Nancy's back and kissed her cheek as they ended their embrace. "I now know why Stan is so crazy about you." They walked to the door. Leah opened and held it. "Talk with you soon."

"Okay. Get some sleep, Leah."

"You too." Leah went out the door and down the walk with her a few steps, watching Nancy walk away til she turned a corner.

Nancy's walk was faster than usual. Her mind was on Leah's kindness, on how Leah wasn't the one Stan wanted, but perhaps needed. A good girl. Woman. Who'd learned, who knew how to love. "I don't even try to harness unicorns, Mrs. Thompson. I let 'em run, maybe even break off their own horns, and then be there if they come back. Or maybe not be there. I don't know the future. But I think I know how to love. I make it a habit of studying black men. I have one." But it was what Leah didn't voice, perhaps was unable to articulate, which worried Nancy. She wondered if Rich was worried about their son. Decided to find out. Their son. His father. Her husband. As far as she knew, Richard was faithful to her throughout their marriage. Faithful, meaning he hadn't slept with anyone. Slept with them. Have intercourse with them. Didn't have to sleep with someone else to be unfaithful. No, could just up and leave. Leave. Even if it meant going to the next room, like in their house. She was close to it now. On their block, and she remembered how at first after the split they made love and then went to sleep in their separate rooms. Not even that anymore. His was his. Hers was hers alone. But she still referred to where she slept as "our room." Would always. Always. Be proud of the way their home looked when you entered it. The hardwood floors in the foyer sanded and finished to a deep golden gloss by Stan and herself. The stairs, the walls, all the work that *they* did on this home, which still showed beautifully. . . , but for what? For whom?

"We're going to find out what the hell is the matter with our boy, Rich," she shouted up the stairs.

"What're you talkin' about? Where've you been—out all night?" He emerged from his room and stood in the hallway, looking down at her.

"I ought to yank you down these damn stairs, Rich. I ought to." She climbed the stairs.

"What? Make sense, Nan, I'm getting ready for Sunday School." He was tucking a white shirt into his black dress slacks.

She stood face to face with him. "This here is your damned church, Rich. This here. Your son, me."

"He's grown."

"So are you. And you still don't know what the hell is going on."

"I know I'm going to church today. I'm scheduled to teach the Sunday School lesson."

"I just left Leah's house, Rich, and even she doesn't know what the hell is happening with him. He's always called me, even when he's sleeping over somewhere. Always."

"Well, always has changed. You can't baby him any more than you already have." Turning away from her, he retreated into the bedroom.

She followed. "You're always going back in your room, or to church; you're always leaving."

"I know." He went to the bed and picked up his black and white tie.

"You're not going anywhere today until you listen to me. I

swear, Rich, you walk down those steps, and when you return this mother will be nothing but ashes. I'll burn it down."

"No, you won't."

At his words, she pushed him, and he fell backward against the bed, but she stumbled also, bouncing off him and into the massive mahogany dresser adjacent to the bed. She fell to the floor. Her side hurt like hell, yet she pushed away his outstretched hand and used the dresser as a crutch. "Don't you dare touch me, Rich."

"You won't stop me from going to church, and you won't burn down the house."

"The house, the house; can't you even bring yourself to call it `mine' or `yours' or `ours'? *The*, as though it's some foreign object. This house is ours, Rich, *ours*! Don't you remember when we selected it together? How we scraped together the down payment by selling our car and riding the bus for a year? How we looked for something we could afford, but could also grow into? Don't you remember, Rich? Don't you know that this house is the only thing, besides Stan, that kept me from leaving you time after time? And then, when Stan grew up, don't you know, man, that I stayed because of this house? Our house!" She sat on the bed. "Our home was supposed to be our place of contentment during these years, Rich, these years we're supposed to be experiencing milk and honey. Years I sanded those railings for, you painted walls for. These terrible, messed up years, when instead of being safe in each other's love, we live alone. Rich, I've got an idea, why *don't* you get out? You want to go to Sunday School, go live in the church. Eat your meals in the church basement. Why don't you just go down those damned stairs with more than the clothes on your back and the Bible in your hand; why don't you pack all your stuff, your sanctimonious stuff, and go the hell to church. And stay there. I'll help you." She leapt up and yanked the spread and sheets off his bed, throwing them in his face. "You bastard." She rushed into her room, slamming the door behind her.

At first, he couldn't move. Could not. Because she hadn't screamed like that in years. He bent to the floor to pick up the white sheets and bedspread. Stayed, tarried there. Felt in his pockets. Pulled out their contents. In his left pocket, two ten dollar bills. Thirteen cents, a dime and three pennies. He put the money back in his pocket. In his right, keys to the car, job, house. Keys to the footlocker, his. Hope chest, hers. Were they still locked? He knew what was in his. His parents' pictures and mementoes from high school. And from service days, his uniforms, revolver, and bullets. Hers, too, he knew. Wedding albums, from both of hers. And death notices, her mom's, dad's, Roy's. But not just photo albums—records. By Dinah Washington. Just those.. Nancy's "Lady D." Their mutual love of music. The only woman he dated who could talk jazz for hours. Hours. They did. Even about Roy, who played bass and performed with some of the "old masters." Her keys were still on his ring. Some of them he never used. Not much in their house was locked. Not even the bedroom doors, just closed. He let the keys drop from his hand and got up. Walked into the red-carpeted hall. Not needing to knock on her, *their* bedroom door, he entered.

* * * * *

It was Sunday morning, quiet, as Stan drove home from Dia's, through downtown. Nine a.m. Only two types of people were downtown this early on a Sunday—the heavenbound and the homeless. He learned this when he thought he was part of the heavenbound, or was striving to be so. Now, he knew that one didn't, couldn't, strive to be; either it happened, or it didn't, and it hadn't happened to him. There was a time when he, like his father, and even his mom, cried, prayed and "tarried." Now, he felt that it wouldn't. Sunday mornings, downtown Buffalo looked either one of two ways—very clean or very dirty. This depended upon whether there was big fun on Saturday night and whether they swept the streets. But it also depended on whom you saw, such as the brothers and sisters with Bibles, waiting on a bus to take them to the Church of Deliverance or St. John Missionary Baptist. While waiting at a light, he noticed a pair of young sisters reading their Bibles or Sunday School lesson. One of the women wore a leather jacket and white dress. She seemed cold and moved from side to side as she peered down the street, presumably looking for the coming bus. Her friend, larger, older looking, was speaking. She was conscious of and playing to their, her, momentary audience, Stan. She closed her Bible and looked into the street for the bus, but directly at his car. She opened her navy trench, adjusting her white sweater and long white skirt. She seemed to recognize his car, him. Smiling, she said something to her friend and took off her white hat, smoothing her hair, which was brushed back and in a tight, neat bun. He didn't know her, but then again, he did, and returned her smile, reflecting on her big white hat, cocked stylishly to the side. Later today, her hat might fly off and be customarily retrieved by Sister usher, when Sunday's rhythm and songs got too good for words, and movement took over. Movement—when she, or her now so-cold sister would feel *fire* and couldn't, sitting or standing still, reach high enough to touch God. So they would stretch, leap, do what Nancy called "the St. Vitus dance," feet shuffling fast, hands happy and waving. It depended upon whom you saw, your view of downtown on a Sunday morning and, really, where you looked. The bus stops were holy on Sundays, as two or three were, invariably, gathered in His name, waiting. But the benches away from the bus stops were the beds of "bums," homeless people who were truly that. It wasn't as easy to pick out the homeless at other times. They mingled within crowds. Weekdays, downtown was filled with workers, and evenings held shoppers, or leftovers from work, folks with homes they didn't want to go to, yet. Weekends signalled times of special events and partying: the cultured hurrying to the opera or a play; revelers; and slow teens huddled, talking about possible play. But on Sunday mornings, only two kinds were out—those who had no beds to go to and those for whom the call of the Lord was stronger than sleep. Sleep. He hadn't gotten much last night.

"You know that I'm in love with you?" he asked Dia when she awakened. He'd watched her sleep for some time.

"You just told me. You always want to have these deep talks when we're in bed, after we make love."

"Isn't that the best time?"

"No, there is no best time."

"Because?"

"Because, based on what you told me, there's no time for us to talk about anything."

"You weren't asleep."

"What was that, Stan, the coward's way out? The chicken-shit way of telling me? Maybe I'm asleep so you haven't really told, and maybe I'm awake, but if I am, it's not the same as facing me."

"I wasn't sure I wanted to tell you, to tell anybody. It's my fight. I don't want you to make it . . . ."

"I won't," she interrupted. "I won't. And I can't understand your plans about killing yourself. And that last bull, about wanting me to have your child. Don't you remember I can't? And if I could, I wouldn't." She was crying, tears streaming down as from a faucet. He reached forward to touch. She jerked away. "No, crazy man, back off. Back off. I need time to deal with this. You talk about plans. I didn't plan on this—any of it."

"Neither did I."

* * * * *

Now home, he was tired but couldn't sleep. It seemed no one was in, or his mom was, dead to the world, but he didn't knock on her door to find out. Roberta Flack, *Quiet Fire*, serenaded him as he worked on a poem for Dia.

> I could tell you things,
> I could give you myself,
> Return to you the world you give me:
> the world of my peter pan reveries at six;
> or I'm fourteen again,
> first paycheck pocketed, headin' home!
> But if I told you these things,
> I'd give you a child
> in this age of abortion
> I'd give you my life
> in this age of death.

Then, he couldn't write anymore, couldn't find more words that fit; finishing was always hard. Like the last turn of the damned race and he was behind, and this one didn't mean much, or did, but he didn't care . . . .

He thought—he didn't know why, wished he could control his thoughts and do otherwise—of one of the times he and his father ever really talked. It, that instance, stuck in his head, or like gum on the soles of his shoes. There not because of his volition but by "accident." It was the first day, no, night, his parents "split," took separate bedrooms. A fight he witnessed through sound—shouts and screams and then the hollowness of silence and then more screams and shouts. Or, worse, a softly-said taunt from the kitchen that he couldn't hear in his bedroom. And he wanted to descend the stairs and join the fray, add his shouts and taunts; or chide them to "stop now"; or, perhaps, just sit at the head of the stairs to hear better, and pray. But he knew this fight was theirs, not his; and that his mom felt the fight was for him too, but it wasn't. He didn't need to fight the man. Once, he hadn't the nerve, but at seventeen, a strong high school senior, he knew he could beat him physically, and so did his father. But he'd never had to hit him for her. The man wouldn't hit her. As a matter of fact, the shouts and screams were hers. His father never screamed or yelled, and if he began to, he caught himself and stopped. No, he wouldn't harm her physically, with his fists. But now, barging through Stan's door was testimony to the harm he was doing. She shouted, again, and ascended the stairs to their room, and then left.

Stan waited for minutes after she left before he tipped down the stairs to the kitchen. His father was talking to himself, God, or the radio, which was turned low.

"No matter how I try, can't make her understand what I'm saying. For one, she's too strong—been that way all her born days—won't change—can't—shouldn't. The problem is the way she sees me." Perhaps his father was addressing him. The older man stared out the dark window as though he were awaiting the morning mail. "Sit down." Stan complied, taking Nancy's place, to Richard's right. His father turned toward him. Their eyes met, forcing Stan to recall a scripture, "The light of the body is the eye." That look reminded him that there can be magic, even momentarily, when eyes meet. Or, there can be nothing but mistrust. If there's magic, it's because the two people, their bodies, minds, see and share a similar light. "The light of the body is the eye." If there's mistrust, it's because there is, or has been, little shared. When the eyes of two people meet—exploring past pupil and iris, color, and stain—all is out front. Mouths and other members of the body can pull off lies. So, too, can the eyes, when they do not meet another's straight on. But when they do, when they meet in the air, no lies are told. "It's different for black women," his father said. "Like *my* dad explained when I was going off to college. Your gram cried and prayed over me, and he said nothing. Then, on the way to the bus terminal, he told me, 'sons never leave. Daughters do, and then they usually come back, but sons never leave.' He also said that in America, 'black women are always old and black men always young.' Do you know what he meant? Huh?"

That night, for the first time, Stan realized that if you've never really talked with someone whom you love, someone with whom talking should be like daily bread, it is tough doing so when you need to, when you have to, when it is apparent that, for whatever reason, they finally want to. He stared out the window for a while, struggling to answer. "I think I know. White people see us as boys."

"But what about your mom, what about how they view our women?" Richard paused, staring from a greater distance, out the window, but also, it seemed, into Stan. "From day one, a black girl is denied her girlhood, just as we are denied our manhood. Black women have to mature fast. They regard her as all sorts of things—experienced, motherly, exotic. And they treat her like she's a woman, whether she's 14 or 40. And that's a heavy burden. We're not ever accorded our manhood, and our women are cheated out of their girlhood. . . ."

Stan began again in his journal. He printed slowly, like a young child concentrating on his homework: "Being black is like being a cancer patient. No, it's not. It's not like *having* something which other people fear, like cancer. No, it's like *being* something which they, white people, fear. The trick is to convince them that you're not black, that you're not what they think black is. You have to live your life trying to convince them that you're not what they think black is. You have to do it with your talk or walk or smile, and sometimes—most of the time?—you don't really know if it works. Are they still just as afraid? Are you still just as "black"? There are two blacks—yours and theirs. Yours—you love; theirs—you hate. Theirs—they fear and loathe; yours—they don't even see. Cancer is the same way. I have to treat it like most white people treat us. I have to treat it as I see it, regard it, not as it pressures me to."

The tape reached its end; he paused, to flip it over, but instead just continued writing. "And how do you achieve manhood when your woman is so strong? Do you have to take it from her? Some black men seem to think so, like my father. And take what? What is there to take? Why did Sheila take our child? Did she? Did she get pregnant to try to save us? Were we lost from the get-go? Is that what every brother fights against, being lost, losing his dreams, like my father? In my father's church, they teach that you should claim your healing. Just claim it. . . . There's a song from my childhood. I can't recall its title, a ballad, with a little boy and an old man. First, the little boy sings:

Old man, old man, is the world really round?
Tell me where in the world can a bluebird be found?
Tell me why is the sky up above so blue?
And when you were a boy, did you cry like I do?

I remember little of the old man's reply, just two lines, the first and the last: *'Little boy, little boy, yes it's true the world's round . . . ./And when I was a boy, yes I cried like you do.'* I loved that song. Maybe I realized as a child that I was to be both the little boy and the old man. Maybe I realized then that I would later remember all of the questions and only some of the answers."

Putting down his pen and pad, he picked up the phone to call Leah. Couldn't Claudia. Dialed. It rang twice. Hanging up, he got the hell out of bed. His father's door was wide open when he arrived home, but he failed to notice it earlier. Now, leaving, he did. His mom's was shut tight when he came in, but it, too, hadn't hit him. Now, it did. And Richard's car in the drive, not at the church.

He walked around his own car. Went into the trunk, got out the towels he carried all the time, to wipe and make it shine. A car he'd helped make, really. Although it was over a decade since it was new, you'd never tell it by the Mustang's look. He'd fixed it. Taken the bad boy apart, right in this mf-ing drive. In that garage. And scraped and sanded and painted its black surface smooth and shiny. Like it was beginning to look this morning. Why hadn't he noticed the dust, the several wet leaves stuck to it? Sunday mornings, he listened to John Coltrane. Driving, he put in a tape, *Transition*. Trane's soothing, melodic, "Dear Lord" was playing. Each time the cut ended, he rewound and replayed it, until he reached his destination.

He parked in a space in front of Leah's apartment. He rang the doorbell. Waited, surveying the complex. Most apartment complexes looked alike. Grass, hedges, walkways, and little patios divided by wooden "fences." They weren't really fences, more like barriers without gates. Openings through which one walked to the patios in the rear of each apartment. One could enter each apartment from the front or the rear. He walked to the rear. Didn't see her car. Hated coming back here. Knew that it was due to the broken asphalt and overflowing garbage bins in the rear. In this complex, the fronts of apartments faced, as did the rears. She gave him a key for her patio door. He never used it, keeping it only in case she or Ray lost theirs. Seldom came back here. He moved the grill to the front when they barbecued. Took out Leah's garbage for her by paying Ray to do it. "My mom believes that it's ridiculous to give children an allowance for doing nothing and then require that they do household chores for free. Paying him for doing chores will help him understand the relationship between working and getting paid."

Sliding back the patio door and drapes, he entered Ray's toyland. Two or three big stuffed animals were spread across the living room rug. Leah didn't believe in doing work twice. Before bed, Ray would have to get the stuff up. Until then, he must keep it out of her way. Stan kicked a pink elephant toward the dining room, sat in a grey, plush recliner across from the TV. Reached over, stretching without leaving the chair, and with both hands lifted a huge brown and orange bear, tossing it in the air and punching it, yelling in English what Kojo uttered in Hausa when he struck anything or won a race: "Why-so-may!" Played with the remote control to the TV; too early for football. A preacher or two. A hunting and fishing show. Couldn't go right back over Dia's. Shouldn't. Thought of other women. . . .

Maxi. After his return from the funeral, they kept in touch. The first card came from her, a "thank you." Evidently, a card designed to be sent in thanks for a gift. A word was whited-over and, in its place, "presence" was written. It read: "Your *presence* was so thoughtful." On the front of the card was a pink, embossed calla lily. The flower reminded him of death. He called upon receipt of the card. After that, more calls, letters, and cards. Like lovers. The lovers that Max laughingly vowed they'd never become. That, alone, gave them something to joke about. Something to help them forget shared sadness. He even went down to see her. Ostensibly, to see the Bahamas under better circumstances and to visit the entire Livingston family. She was living in Max's old place, and Stan used the spare bedroom during his week in Nassau. They boated over to Freeport and Exuma; jogged and played tennis, sometimes with Manny. Stan played the slots; and paid his respects, again, to the family. They visited Max's resting place. It was in a good location, a precipice overlooking the ocean, but viewing it, Stan saw nothing that spoke to how fast Max sprinted, nothing that told how he represented his nation in the Olympics. The plot gave no indication that

Max, while away, wrote and called his mother weekly. The dirt didn't describe how he sent his siblings and nephews t-shirts from every away meet. And so influenced Stan to begin doing the same for Nancy. His headstone told no tales of "four de hard way," *his* relay team. On each side of it were vibrant tropical flowers, purple, white and fuchsia, planted and cared for by Maxi. Yet even they, blowing in a breeze from off the Atlantic, couldn't convey the vibrancy which was Max.

"We rushin'/We rushin'/We rushin'/Through de crowd . . ." They sang, shouted the summer after graduation, through the streets of Toronto. Now, the festival boasted a name, Caribana, and all of the other stuff that happens when a party becomes a commodity. But then, it was just him and Max and a few hundred other black people, diasporan people, singin' Carib songs and dancing the night into existence. He couldn't quite remember; did it begin with them takin' over underground Toronto? Or did it commence on the Toronto Islands with Max playing loud party music: Sparrow or Marley or Jimmy Cliff, too loud, until the loudness, like the beat, became just right. And then grabbin' a pretty black woman by her waist and dancin' as they did that night, up the stairs or elevator, or whatever they climbed, into the cool Canadian night, a night warmed by the colorful, tropical people dancing through the streets. That August in Toronto was the last time he saw Max alive. After a point that night, Stan left Max and Decky and Rod, drinking Barcardi and smoking reefer, took the Ferry from Toronto Islands and walked alone to his hotel room. A few folk were still out, refusing to let the party die. Some waved to him as he walked, others simply stared. All except him were in groups, holding hands, talking, sharing warmth and safety at 2:00, 3:00 in the morning. He felt safe, free. He always did in Toronto, perhaps because of its international flavor, but perhaps because he wasn't in the States. At the time, he'd only traveled to Canada and Mexico, Tijuana, once, a fast trip following a meet in San Diego. Outside of the States, surrounded by black folk from throughout the diaspora, from black countries, he wasn't simply a black American, a second-class citizen anymore, but more a citizen of the world. His great grandfather was never enslaved in *this* country, Canada. Here, he could greet his African and Caribbean brothers, and sisters, with the feeling that the deal was undone, the caged bird had flown the coop and could indeed fly like they. Like Max. Running with Max was just that, rushin' through de crowd, and then flyin', and this grave couldn't show that.

Stan wanted to visit the grave one last time, before he and Maxi went to dinner. His early flight might prevent him from doing so tomorrow morning. The ocean reflected the moonlight. No boats were on it. It shone like black glass. Although they were dressed for dinner, he and Maxi sat on the grass by the grave, holding hands. It was peaceful, cool, serene, like the cool Stan felt from the breeze he made when he began to run, to warm up. He just wanted to sit by the grave "till that great gettin' up morning." Wanted to stay and wait for his friend to rise. No, wanted him still alive. That night, he and Maxi ate dinner at a little bar that was Max's favorite. The men there remembered Stan from the funeral and stuffed him with food. Asked him question upon question about his track times, about "four de hard way." And the basketball "tournament" Max and he waged for four years. Was the tally really thirty-six to one in Max's favor? They wanted him to leave Maxi "for awhile" and hang with them. "That gal ain't really showed you Nassau, mon. You done come here twice, and still ain't seen da right spots. Da spots Maximillian woulda taken ya to." Stan declined. He did see the spots that meant the most: this hill, this grave. Maxi. Max's family. His apartment. Stan still regarded it as that, not merely because of his bro's photos and trophies inside it. The apartment was all windows, surrounded outside by palms and other tall greenery. Windows, and because the palms blocked them from the sun's rays, they reflected like mirrors. Like Max, who, more than anyone, saw Stan as he desired to be seen, reflected him clearly.

"Think you can find your way to your room with the lights out? Sometimes I like it like this," she asked.

"Yeah, I can."

"Good."

All during the week, they stayed up late like kids at camp, sitting in one another's room, drinking tea or wine, sharing cookies or cheese or a case of "the hungries." The apartment was hot because they turned off the air conditioning prior to leaving this afternoon. Once in his pajamas, he set up the Wari board for their final game. The loser tonight must submit to being tickled by the victor. . . . She entered naked. He wasn't prepared for this. She introduced him to several beautiful Bahamian sisters, friends of hers or Max or just, "women I thought you'd like to meet." Naked, Maxi's black body was reflected in the windows, surrounding him. Three, four, five, naked Maxis, the sister of his dead, drowned best friend, summoned him. Mesmerized, he stared, touching the top button of his pajama top, which he always wore open. He didn't know whether to undress or button up. Then, he looked away, toward a bookshelf which held a snapshot of him and Max breaking the tape together, a photo finish, at the NCAA quarterfinals their senior year. He wanted to hug her once she reached the bed, standing so close his breath could cool her skin, or warm it. He didn't breathe. Couldn't. He laid his head on her firm, soft stomach and closed his eyes, resisting the urge to kiss her stomach or lick it. "No."

"This is what Max would have wanted, Son. Us, together." Her hands stroked the nape of his neck, moved down to his shoulders. "He loved you so much. Every time I come into this room, see that snapshot of you two, look through Max's photo albums, I realize how much you meant to one another."

"No, Maxi, this isn't us. `We' were just a game Max and I used to play. He didn't want us together."

"He did." She removed her hands slowly. "He did." She turned away. His eyes were magnetized to her shape, her black body, as she moved toward the doorway. Stopping there, beautiful, she turned to him, "Max did." Then, she left.

In the morning, Manny took him to the airport, saying just that "Maxi had errands to run."

* * * * *

. . . He went into Leah's kitchen to use the phone. Didn't know the damn number. Remembered the area code, 809, and the first three digits, 323. That was enough. Got the number, after jiving with the operator. Loved talking with sisters with accents. Recognized Maxi's "hello," but asked for her anyway.

"This is she."

"This is Stan, you know, Son."

"I knew your voice, Son."

"I shouldn't have rejected you. I regret having done so."

"Yes."

"I didn't want to ruin our friendship. And I didn't know if you wanted to make love because of Max . . . maybe we ought to try and see what can happen between us."

"It's been years since you came down, Son, since Max passed."

"I know, I know you haven't heard from me since then. I sent your mom cards a couple of Christmases." He paused, wanting to say what was on his mind, in his heart, but not being sure he should. "I look at my trophies and scrapbooks, Maxi, and I still miss your brother."

"Your brother, too. I know you loved him."

"I love you," he blurted. "And have probably done so since you came to Buffalo in your brother's wallet. Your pictures, you know?" He paused, counting to three, then four, thinking of how her brother would have handled this. "I'm not married any longer, and . . . "

"I heard."

"I don't know, Maxi, I miss that cat. He was more than . . . ."

"I know, he was more than a friend," again she finished his sentence for him. "But that don't mean you should be calling me up and talking romance. You didn't want me years ago. Besides, what make you think I been waiting for some big, strong American to come rescue me from Paradise?"

Her words sounded like something Max would say. "So I guess we're not going have a little Max together," he laughed.

"Not unless youse talking about a drink of some kind, chile."

"No."

"Besides," she continued, "you were right that night, it wasn't us, Son. It was Max and the night and our sorrow. We shared a lot when you were down here, Son. That brought us so close together, and I guess I kinda wanted the fantasy that we all used to kid about. Max and you and me. But Max . . ."

". . . is dead," he said, taking *her* words, "and we were never more than a recurring dream."

"Which might have turned into a nightmare." She interrupted. "I don't think I'll ever marry, Son. If I did, it would be to someone like you, but look at you, you couldn't make it work with, . . . I don't know her name."

"Neither do I. . . . Sheila, her name is Sheila. But I *don't* even know where she is. I guess she's still alive. He paused, waiting for Maxi to speak. Then, to fill the silence, he continued. "I'm getting in shape again, feel like I can run anchor for four de' hard way."

"But you can't."

"Maybe not," he admitted, agreeing aloud but not in his heart. He reflected on last night with Dia, and the nights he and Max would party, party, and his blown night with Maxi, the smooth, black invitation of her body. He recalled her elegy for Brother Max. But she was naked while reciting it.

This time, she interrupted his reverie. "I've got to go, Son."

"OK, but I would like to come down for a visit," he inquired, lying, knowing he didn't love her, although he did perhaps need her, need what she symbolized.

"Fine. You're welcome."

"Oh, and do you know how to track down KK?"

"No, he came through, left some numbers with Manny, but they're no good. Manny tried them about a month ago."

"Doesn't anybody stay in one . . . "

". . . place anymore," she again finished what he began. "No," she laughed, "especially you Americans, or as Max would say, you damn black Canadians."

"Bye, Maxi, give Mom Livingston my best."

"Bye."

She hung up the phone. He didn't. Instead, he began tapping the receiver against the kitchen counter, humming; humming and tapping out the rhythm to "Independence Bahamas." Then, taking a second to remember it, he dialed Alton's number.

"Hello."

"Hey Ton."

"Son! Son. Long time, man! What's up?"

"Nothing, nostalgia. I was just talking with Maxi, and I wanna try to track down KK. Know where he is?"

"No idea. He was living in Chi-town last time I talked with him, about a year ago. Said he was going over to London to see some woman. He could be anywhere between Accra and L.A. You know the cities where he hangs. Anyplace where there's a critical mass of Nigerians: Chicago, L.A., D.C., Atlanta, the Apple. I'm surprised he hasn't hit Nickel City in awhile. Too bad Max isn't around. Call him, and he'd tell you where we were, what we were doing. . ."

" . . . and who we were doing it with," Stan cut in.

"Or who we wanted to do it with."

It felt good, good to talk with folks who could finish his sentences. "Ton, we have got to all get together. I miss all the stuff we used to get into. The all-night raps about simple stuff, the late night runs for food."

"I know."

"Ton, I don't want us to get together just when there's a ceremony of some kind. For a minute, I thought about proposing to Maxi."

"Well, I hope you didn't. You just got out of one of those not too long ago."

"I know. Don't be 'in love,' just love, right?"

"Right, so you remember something we taught you."

"We? Where do you get off with this 'we' mess? That was Max."

"According to you, everything was you or him. Look, man, the best way to find someone you're after is to retrace their steps as you know them. And if that doesn't work, retrace your own, to where you last saw them. You could, of course, work forward, if you know their future plans. You have KK's favorite cities. Which one was the last place you saw him?"

"Here, the Nickel."

"What you need is seven people."

"Seven people?"

"Right, haven't you heard, Son, that you can locate anybody with just seven people? I imagine, though, that it has to be the *right* seven people, not seven random people. Anyway, it seems to me that today you've talked with two of your seven. Five to go."

"Thanks. I forgot you minored in philosophy and in running off at the jibbs."

"Free advice, my man. Some people have to pay for my words."

"The crazy ways of white folks."

"Glad I'm not one of 'em."

"No, paleface, you're not. Watch yourself."

"That's all I've been doing lately. I'm not with anybody right now. And I've been attending church, an AME Zion not far from where I teach, and they jam! I'm also helping out a local high school track coach, mainly with the sprinters and relay teams. So tell Nancy and hug her for me. And let's get together, soon."

"We will, Ton, *with* KK. Take care, man. Later."

"Yeah, later."

Hanging up the receiver, Stan decided to wait for Leah; exercise while he waited.

* * * * *

The silk of Nancy's robe was damp with his sweat. They made love—it'd been so long!—and now, they fit like spoons. Her behind was nestled in his mid-section. Their legs made parallel v's. His left arm was her pillow; his right, her banner, as it was on top of the sheet covering them. Just a sheet, but she wasn't cold. They weren't. She dabbed the perspiration on his arm. He slept. As far as she knew, Richard remained faithful to her during their "separation." Faithful, meaning he hadn't screwed another woman. She looked at the window, *at*, not out, it, as the white blinds were down and only slightly open, just enough for her to guess the hour, mid-morning, 10:00, 10:30.   Afterward, they'd both dozed. No Sunday School this morning. She wanted to turn and kiss his forehead, neck, chest, all of him, without waking him. She was always the one living on "front street," giving the most, being the bluntest. He had a way of saying a lot but not telling you a damned thing. But she would pop, jump like hot, greased kernels of corn for him. And not care that he knew she would. That, for her, was being faithful. She wondered if he was, in the same way. If their bedrooms were used as indicators, he at least continued thinking of them as a couple. His present room, the guest room, mirrored hers in many ways. He changed nothing since their split. Even the little things were still the same. White, one hundred percent cotton percales, covered by white down-filled comforters. Fresh flowers every Friday for the round corner tables, a combination of pink roses and white carnations, with baby's breath. Always twelve. The nightstand next to his bed held, like hers, three things—a brass lamp, a clock radio, and a box of white tissues. "White walls, sheets, and tissues—never go wrong with them." Sharing these words, originally her mother's, with Rich and later Stan also meant showing them what one would do with color. "You should've been an artist." Where were they when Rich said that? On one of their earliest dates? Shopping, perhaps, browsing at AM&A's or Sattler's, where she worked for years, was the first black commissioned saleswoman. And eventually gained the position she coveted, designing displays and decorating. She decorated BB's. . . . Rich was beginning to stretch. Time to get up. He would want to make the morning service.

She wanted him to stay with her this morning. She wanted for them to together greet their troubled son. But she simply lay there, silently, as she watched him dress, in his uniform: black worsted wool suit, white shirt, grey silk tie, black spit-shined shoes. He always knelt and prayed before leaving the house to go anywhere. She watched as he did it this morning, beside the bed. She'd withdrawn her hand as he reached for it prior to beginning his prayer. This time, it wasn't going to be so easy. They were great lovers together, like she heard him say about tennis, the better the partner's game, the better one's own. Theirs together, for sex and for show, was always great. But besides that, no, not even now. As she watched him pray, she evicted him, put him out of the house. He was back, alone, riding in the car listening to the radio. He was singing one of his favorite songs, "Deep River," "This Little Light," or "I'm Glad." He was listening to a Sunday morning sermon. He wasn't kneeling next to her, his manicured, black hand flat on her white sheet, where her hand left it. He wasn't going back to Sunday School, the church, the God, she once confessed to him she was jealous of. No, he wouldn't do that again, hit and run again, come down to her room for *some*, after so long, and then simply leave? Saints didn't do that. Nice boys, what she derisively called him when they first met and she told him to leave her alone, didn't do what he'd done to her time and again. Nice boys, like the nice boy he seemed to be that she promised to corrupt if he let her, didn't play with the hearts of fast, experienced girls like her. Nice boys, husbands, didn't leave the wives they'd never divorce like he was leaving her this morning, with new questions and no strength to ask for answers. She turned over as he rose, putting her back to him like so many earlier times that their movement to separate rooms made sense because they weren't really sleeping together anyway, just in the same bed, and this little bit of togetherness didn't make things better. He was still going to speed to church in his black Lincoln and sharp clothes and manners. She was still going to BB's today, or tonight.

* * * * *

Leah's kitchen was her haven. She came here to "sit and smoke and make meals and pig out and party by myself." It was seldom that she invited guests to join her in here. The front half of the kitchen was filled with the conventional. White appliances, stainless steel, white cabinets. A blue formica-topped table. Four wooden chairs, in a matching antique blue. The rear half of the kitchen contained mirrored walls and was divided from the front by a multi-colored striped rug. A navy love seat and a matching occasional chair faced each other on the rug. An oval-shaped coffee table was between them. Just off the rug and against one of the mirrored walls were her stereo, records, and tapes. In order to exercise, Stan rearranged her furniture. He needed both portions of the room. The hard linoleum for sit-ups and push-ups, the carpeted area for jumping and running in place. He was used to looking at himself when exercising. Stretching—and then he was going to do one hundred each of the sit-ups and push-ups, while Marvin Gaye crooned. He wasn't stopping until she arrived, no matter how long. Leah never worked out, said she didn't have to, she was a mother. She would laugh, "I have a rambunctious boy who keeps me hopping, I work eight hours a day, five days a week, and I can go to BB's and shake my bootie. So what do I need a workout for? My life is a workout." Marvin was his favorite because every word the man sang *worked out*. "Let's get it on. Let's get it on. Let's love, baby."

The blue and white patterned floor was so immaculate he could complete his bends and stretches with a kiss of the linoleum. "Let me love you." They made love on it. "Please get it on." Started in the carpeted area—and rolled, moved together till the linoleum was moist, sticky with their sweat. Lying on it now, he wasn't surprised at how clean or how white the counter tops were. What surprised him about Leah, about sisters like her, was how she did it, everything. Like now, she was at her mom's church, keeping Ray in tow as the minister rambled. Looking as fine, probably in a blue or black designer suit, as when she left her mirror this morning. The type of sister who left black men awestruck and white folks envious. Who kept their kids and kitchens clean and full while they, in well-dressed poverty, looked like the million they'd never get. Who were the reason there was no such phrase as "poor black trash,"—because poor black women were such treasures; and they were also the reason he'd never "played in the snow." They and something Marvin said in an *Ebony* interview, about feeling an obligation toward black women. "Stay babe, please stay. Stan believed that the Oedipus Complex was, because of such women, the black man's complex.

"If I should die tonight," Marvin wailed about dying and loving and knowing his lover, dying differently because of that knowledge, Stan finished his stretches and began his sit-ups. Kept his stomach in, tight. Hated doing these, but loved the results. So many people did them wrong. Leah. During their first months he kidded her about her tiny midriff bulge and asked her to do sit-ups. She did a couple of times when she accompanied him to the gym. But eventually she admitted she didn't believe in exercising. And argued that his momma was the only woman with whom he wouldn't find fault. He paused between sit-ups, holding his bent knees between his arms. His mom was one bad lady. Was what she always called him, the best. Yes, there were times, he wanted to hurt his father. And marry his mom?—no, but something like it. Just give her something, somebody better.

He was into the thirties of his jumps when he heard her enter. While singing along with Marvin on "Get To This," his favorite on the album. He sang it to her once. Leah entered the kitchen and stood just inside the doorway, staring. He stopped jumping and danced toward her, kissing her forehead and continuing along with Marvin, but facing her, "you're so fine. So petite, awh, candy sweet." She turned her face away from his kiss, so that he kissed her hair. She walked to the stereo and turned it off. In her navy worsted wool suit, his favorite. Damn, she looked good. At times, for reading and night driving, she wore glasses. She wore them now. He loved her in them. When she turned from the music box to face him, he began to say how fantastic she looked, but she beat him.

"What're you doing here, Stan?"

"Exercising. Waiting for you. Getting it on with my man Marvin."

"Looks like you were having fun. And I wouldn't mind it, Stanford, but we haven't exactly been keeping company recently." She strode toward him, Marvin Gaye tape in her right hand, tapping it hard into the palm of her left. "Know what I mean? And for you to then just show up, and not even *show up*, but *be* here unannounced when I come home from somewhere, well, Stan, this is just too much." She tossed the tape to the floor.

"Didn't you just come from . . . ," he started to say, but the look she gave him stopped him from going that way. He went another. "Lee, I wanted to talk with you, so I let myself in and waited."

"Obviously."

"I made a couple of long-distance calls, Maxi and Alton— Nassau and Seattle."

"I know you'll pay me. I'm not even going to ask why you came over here and made the longest possible damn calls you could."

He was tired, not from the earlier exercises, but from standing in the middle of her kitchen, talking like this. "Where's the kid?" Saying this, he bent down and reached around her leg, to retrieve the tape. Quickly, her foot went back, simultaneously kicking the cassette from his reach and stepping on his hand.

"Leave it down there, Stan. Ray's at momma's."

"Lee, what's your problem?"

She ignored his question. "I'm taking Ray to a birthday party this evening. Diane's son, Jesse, is six today."

"I don't want to go with. . . ."

" . . . I wasn't going to ask you to. I was going to say that I have a lot to do, and I'm tired, and you're making me more tired." She opened the black patent purse slung from her arm, took out a pack of cigarettes and lighter.

"I thought you were cutting down."

"I am. Two a day. This is my first."

"You know you always have a smoke before bed." He put his hand on hers holding the pack.

"Let go of my hand." She looked at his hand touching her. "Now."

"I'm trying to do this for your good," he said as he pulled away.

"You haven't done anything for my good since I've known you. Or for your good, either. You're bad for both of us." She moved away from him, to the rear of the kitchen. "Stan, I don't know why you came over here. Why you let yourself in. What was the urgency?" She was placing her pieces of furniture in their usual spots.

"Let's go in the living room and talk." He walked behind her.

She persisted at her tasks. She kicked off her patent pumps, and set her purse on top the stereo. "We don't need to, Stan. I know you're seeing somebody, but that's not even it. Cause if I cared, I could get you back. You don't believe it, but I could. I don't want *us*. You think I used to call you all the time to try to keep you. I did that because you needed a friend. A friend. Stanford Thompson. Big man. Everybody knows him. Jock. All-whatever. So what? I could look at you and see how lonely you were. From the first day we met I could. I just cared, Stan.

That's all. I never really thought we were going to get together. Never. Wouldn't have wanted it if you'd asked. Really. All I wanted to show you was that I cared." She stopped, went to a counter where her cigarette hung. Puffed on it, put it back, leaned against the counter, so close to her cigarette that if she moved an inch the wrong way she would burn a hole in her suit. "All I wanted to show you, Stan, was that you have a friend, a phone number, a house you can count on. Our being a pair, lovers, I never figured on that. Never." She picked up the cigarette butt, puffed, holding its smoking edge between slender fingers with fire-red nails.

With two steps, he crossed the room, confronting her. Shaking his head, he opened his arms to embrace her.

"No." She turned away, flicking the butt in his face with one hand and opening a kitchen drawer with the other. She pulled out a knife. "Get out."

"Are you crazy, Lee?" He jerked his head away from the flying cigarette butt.

"No, you're crazy. Now get out, Stan." She threw the knife at him, grazing his forearm, drawing blood. "I'm calling momma, then the cops if I need to."

"Okay, fine." He picked up the knife, tossed it in the sink, then grabbed his sweats from one of the chairs. "There're some things I need to do." Shaking his head, he turned and left. Goodbye, Leah." She didn't reply, but he heard her crying as he opened the front door. He paused, looking back through the kitchen doorway, toward the sounds of her crying and dialing the phone. Seeing only her stockinged feet as the rest of her body was blocked from his view, he wanted to turn back to Leah and say something, anything, but what? He walked out the front door into the morning. He conversed with her as he walked away. "You know, Leah, that I love you."

"I know."

"I understand your anger, Lee. I haven't been totally honest."

"I know."

"And even though you mentioned that I'm seeing someone else, that's not the problem. The problem is you're too perfect, everything that you can give me, you have. And that's why it's hard to leave you, leave us. But there are some things that I need, Lee, that you just can't give me, and no matter how long we stay together that won't change."

"I know."

Once at his car, he discovered that his keys weren't on him, but he didn't want to return to Leah's to look for them. Leah. Maxi. Dia. Three women. He could only have one, but he really needed something from each, three in one. Leah was steady and pretty and prompt, a sure bet. She looked good on his arm, and she *did* good at home. If he was smart, he'd turn around and kneel at her feet. But he wasn't, not when it came to women. He picked Sheila, hadn't he? Maxi gave him soul, spirit, connections. It was like forever being with the best of his past, a time he wished had never ended. Sheila was going to make it big. He'd read about her some day, see her photo on the cover of *Essence* and say to himself, "I had her." But that was a lie and, truth be told, he married her because he could, because it was obvious she was going to one day be somebody, and he wasn't sure, in spite of "everything he accomplished," that he was. Dia was the type of woman he and Max would've competed over, even more than a Sheila. Yeah, he and Max would've looked at her, listened to her, wanted her, because she was the type of sister whom money, or the promise of prosperity, couldn't buy. She might love you, but she would still "dump your ass," still tell you what to do with your b.s., and to grow up. . . . Three in one—that couldn't happen, but maybe, just maybe, Dia, *his* Lady Day, could.

* * * * *

Leah hung up the phone. Went to the sink and turned on the faucet. Picked up the knife and a wash cloth. Wet the wash cloth, wrung it, and wiped with the cloth. Then, using a towel, she wiped it dry until it gleamed, till it was a mirror in which she could see her face. She let the water run and wiped the kitchen counters and everything on them: first with the wet rag, then the dry. She swept the floor. Moved the kitchen table back to where it was before he rearranged it. The chairs, love seat, coffee table, each piece of furniture, were moved. She took time to get them in the exact spots in which they had been. Turned off the faucet when she finished with the furniture. Called her mother, asked her to bring Ray home. Retrieved her overnight bag from the hall closet, walked into Ray's room, to get him a change of clothes and a pair of pj's. In the bathroom, she gathered the toiletries each would need for a brief trip. Once in her own room, she finally shed the clothes she wore to church. She chose two outfits and a nightgown for herself. For the party, a pair of blue jeans and her blue Spelman sweatshirt. She never attended college, but Spelman would have been her choice. She packed her black leather slacks and newest sweater, purchased at Saks during her last trip to New York City. Originally priced at $250, she paid $49. Though they looked new, the leather slacks were five years old, almost as old as Ray. She admired herself, in bra and panties, in the full-length mirror on the closet door. She had about a half-hour before their arrival. Leah lay down on the bed. If she dozed, their entrance would awaken her. Sunday evenings used to be her and Stan's time. He still had her house key. She'd call Nancy in a week or so and ask that she get it for her. She didn't want to have the lock changed. She closed her eyes. Ray would be so surprised. Niagara Falls after the party. Tomorrow, they would play hookey from work and school. She made a mental note to remember to get Jesse's present out of the hall closet when, upon leaving, they got their coats, her long black leather, and Ray's quilted ski jacket and knit cap. It would be frigid at the Falls. Tonight they'd eat burgers in the revolving restaurant atop Seagram's tower. He'd been begging her to do that. And tomorrow they'd walk around the Canadian side, since Ray was anxious to tour the haunted house. Hopefully, he wouldn't be too scared. Actually, they both were chickens, and they'd probably end up walking through it clinging to each other.

PART II

Proverbs 4:3

For I was my father's son,
tender and only beloved
in the sight of my mother.

CHAPTER
4
That the Race

Stan was glad to be headin' home on foot, walk a little, run a little. It was a cross-country type of day, just cold enough so he would barely break a sweat, but sufficiently warm that nothing heavy was needed. He wasn't in love with Leah, hadn't ever been, but he needed her. And had welcomed her, like he welcomed a strong breeze on his back at the end of a race. Leah helped him make it past the memories of losing Sheila and the baby; past the pain of Max's drowning; past the dreams he'd deferred to thoughts of death. No, he wasn't *in love* with Leah, whatever that meant. Max used to say "don't fall in love, just love." But he did love Leah, would always, for what she gave to him, herself and her son. Leah helped him make it to Dia, but he still hadn't made it to himself.

Thirty-two was too damn old to be this way. It was too damn old to be living at home with his parents, even if he *was* doing it to look out for his mom. It was too damn old to still be running to reach "the kingdom of adulthood"—the place, the act, the situation which, when one reaches, says to oneself and all, "I've made it." Sheila had; so had Leah; and Dia didn't care. But for black men, making it was hard, almost impossible, take it from his father. They usually weren't accorded manhood 'til death, martyrdom. Neither chronology nor graduation did it. Neither did serving—country, God, family . . . wife. Marriage didn't do it, nor did owning a white house, with fences, on a good street. No, not even when they won, as he, medals, trophies. Physical strength didn't do it. Not even for some of *them*, Ton. Big white boy who won big, the American way. Beaten blacks at their own game—running. But he was regarded as a mutant, homo. Guy could run his ass off. He was born that way. *That* way. People aren't born one way for life. Birth brought with it few irrevocable sentences but death. Death. And life after it? Maybe. His father believed . . . in what? "In America, black women are forever old and black men forever young." "All we have is ourselves and our women." He loathed his father, in the same way he did Sheila. Yet his father taught him deep, abiding lessons, although by negation and a "laissez faire" stance, like his father's words to his mom after he returned from a grammar school field trip. His fifth grade class, taught by Mrs. Butler, a proud black woman who shared with her students worlds which hadn't opened so easily for her. The children were studying famous visual artists and artwork and now, finally, they would view the work of some real artists, in Buffalo's Albright-Knox Art Gallery. Twenty-four anxious, rambunctious black children, led by their teacher, marched single file into the gleaming glass and marble structure. Their childish chatter manifested their mood—anxious and aware that they were someplace special, if only because Mrs. Butler believed so and because they were excused from classes for the day. But their first greeting wasn't the sight of a Van Gogh or a Winslow Homer or a Whistler, but the sound of a white man, one who saw whiteness as territory and their blackness and childish chatter as trespass, and who whispered loudly, "What is this, a zoo? Look at all the monkeys." Later during the same field trip, while the class quickly ascended a set of stairs in quest of more art treasures, a white woman—whom they quickly passed, and in whose eyes they were not *children*, but four and twenty blackbirds, *escaped*—sneezed and said, "I'm allergic to niggers." Upon returning home, Stan recited to his mom the details of the trip, what they saw and what he remembered most, even to this day. She sat down with him at the kitchen table, over chocolate chip cookies, his favorite, and milk, and explained, "Son, some white people are just ignorant. What they wanted to do was to drive your class out of there, to make you feel inferior to their sorry asses. Excuse me, to them. But you're not, you hear me? They probably think that Van Gogh and Rembrandt are only for white people." They discussed at length the field trip, including the exhibits, but repeatedly they returned to discuss "those ignorant asses" his mom couldn't help cursing. His father never addressed the incident with him directly, although Stan overheard what he said when Nancy relayed the story. "Nan, the end of every black kid's childhood occurs when they see how white people regard them. I hate that it happened, but it was good that it did."

No, he couldn't loathe or blame his father, or Sheila, for anything; perhaps they helped to better equip him for being a black man, who, according to his father, was blessed or cursed with perpetual youth and a black woman—a woman whom Stan had but did not have. A woman, like Sheila, whom he couldn't seem to find; or Leah, whom he didn't want; or his mom, whose level of love he couldn't reciprocate; or Dia, whom he couldn't comprehend. He quickened his pace to a jog.

* * * * *

Nancy thought of her husband at church. She was still a member there, had been for years. Their marriage took place there. She recalled the sunlight slanting through the stained glass, the regal presence of the plush red carpet under her feet, her slight wobble as she first walked toward Rich. And Rich in black tails, waiting at attention, like a sentry. Staring at her, smiling. She walked in white. Long, flowing, white lace gown. A tiara with a veil which, she was certain, couldn't hide the satisfaction on her face, the joy. The two of them decided upon white for her dress; black and white, for his tux, like today. Today, she was in the draped in the whiteness of sheets made damp with their sweat. Today, he returned in black to the house of the Lord. She guessed, no, knew, that she wasn't to him what he hoped for then. But she'd tried her best. Then, so many doubted the match. Bright, good Richard Thompson, with a girl who'd been *had* before. Married to, a fool for, that crazy Roy Williams. She was desperate now, they said. He was doing her a big favor. Settling. He could go far, but not with her. She'd hold him back. What did she have to offer him, who, after returning home from the service, matriculated to Syracuse and had completed all but one year? Who received scholarships to three schools, Canisius, Niagara, and Syracuse, and probably could have gone anywhere if he decided to look farther from home. One of the city's best athletes, a star track man, but who attended Syracuse on an academic scholarship. One who could become anything, doctor, teacher, lawyer. Some said he was called to the ministry, to preach the Gospel. Now this. He should be with a college girl, someone his equal. Whose family background was better. Her people weren't even good Christians. They married in his family's church. But his was hers, she said. They allowed that she *was* sweet. Pretty. A hard worker, with two jobs. A salesgirl at Sattlers and a waitress at Deco on weekends. Was she pregnant? Rich Thompson was a young deacon who didn't drink, smoke, or dance. But this marriage made one wonder. *Her* second. She hastened her first to the grave; and now had bewitched poor Rich by playing like she loved the

Lord. She was the reason he was backsliding. They danced on their wedding night; she better than he. Saints didn't dance, except to the Lord. Well, when they danced, as husband and bride, it was worship. To her, worship was everything one did. The skeptics watched and waited for it to end. Their dance did, with a final spin accompanied by an arpeggio of ivories with strings. Their marriage began in the flesh that night. To wait, his idea. He carried her from the car, taking off his black tails, wrapping them around her, to protect her from the chill. Carried her, because some traditions make sense, he said. Not to prove his strength, even though he opened the apartment door in the dark without putting her down, but to give her what she deserved. Just doing things right, he said, like waiting till that night. He knew that it wouldn't be her first. But it would be *theirs*. Theirs, he and his slender tree. He called her that because she stood next to a sapling, washing her uncle's car when he spied her. "A good wind would have bent you both over, but *you'd* have continued working." After Roy's death, she moved in with her aunt and uncle, in a house down the street from the apartment building where Rich lived, the summer prior to his upcoming senior year. He'd moved out of his parents' house. They spent most of that summer together. He just walked down to say hello because she was the only young woman on the block. He watched her, always rushing—to the bus stop in front of his building; sometimes driving away fast in her uncle's car. He kidded her, that first day, that people who drove like her shouldn't. She agreed, adding: "Ever." She shared his loves, clothes and music. Showed him how to dance, bop; gave him his first Billie Holiday album. "Strange Fruit." "God Bless the Child." "Crazy He Calls Me." Schooled him regarding why she considered "Lady D," Dinah Washington, special. He loved her in work clothes. She looked like a little kid whose mom made outfits big, to grow into. A brown bean pole with a shape. He shared his love of music. How he taught himself to play the piano by ear. The chords he knew best were the ones he picked up in church. Always coming back to them when he improvised, played jazz. He loved Monk, whom she also hipped him to. She opened up for him worlds the church denied . . . she opened up for him, that night, the drapes sheltering *her*, his slender tree. She worked. That night, he did. Slowly, with patience. Their garments came off like they were all they owned. Next to the bed, one pile, black and white, rising like a steeple. He made love with her like he danced, whispering "are you?" and "if this?" while he moved, on her, with her. Inside her.

* * * * *

He wanted his wife, his son, and his God. That was all he ever wanted. "You give your life away to people." Rich was discussing his marriage, Nancy and the expectant baby, with Gwen, his favorite cousin, his closest friend. The church's best soloist, with a range from second soprano down to wherever she desired. Could pray. Teach a class, using precept and example. She'd traveled everywhere, trying to become "the next Bessie Smith." Toured with several bands for almost six years. She hadn't become the next Bessie, "but not because I didn't try. I lived that part of my life. I *lived* it. Did everything I needed to do to be me." Now, "being me" meant "running for Jesus." In their denomination, if not for her gender, Gwen would've been a pastor, a bishop. But women weren't allowed to preach. One of the recurring lines in her testimonies was, "Yes, I'm running for Jesus. And I want yawl ta follow! I'll help ya keep up," boomed with a rich resonance which impelled you to take her up. Rich, during his teens, did just that.

"Rich, honey, you give your life away to people." Gwen repeated herself, this time standing up, all 6'2" of her. They were the same height, but she looked down at him as he sat in her porch swing. "You knew that when you married her. Should have. All your questions now, ain't about how you surprised 'cause this baby wasn't planned. I don't even know if you care 'bout what it's gonna do to yawl's marriage. You wonderin' how you gonna get to your dreams now." Standing behind him now, she pushed the swing gently. He enjoyed the motion. "Rich, you just gonna have to get to them in the midst of your life. I know you wanna finish college, preach, get a law degree. A preaching attorney, sanctified. My little cousin." She pushed the swing, as it had almost stopped. "Ever since I baby-sat you, I knew you would be somebody special. Remember Mrs. Cheatum's 'Good News Club'? You was the youngest there but always at the head of the class. Like a little prophet, always wantin' to have your say, always feelin' it was important. She made you feel special, Sister Cheatum did, always goin on about your noble walk and intelligent look. She used to take your hand, lead you up front, and say, `this baby is destined for greatness.' `Greatness,' I mean, how did she know that when you weren't more than three or four? *Greatness.*" Gwen stopped the swing's motion, grabbing and holding both chains by which it was suspended. "Rich, greatness ain't just getting up in front of folks, using that voice of yours, wearin' sharp clothes." She chuckled and pinched his shoulder. "Naw, you can be great tryin' to live your dreams with the life you got. So just reconcile yourself to now. Somebody told me that near the end of my singing career. Don't stop pursuing your dreams, Cous, but don't ever blame her or that baby, once it's born, for things you don't do."

A preacher, an attorney. He desired to represent God to his people; and represent his people to an unjust system. As Gwen proclaimed proudly, a sanctified preacher and an attorney—what a combination! It was, for Rich, a dream combination. One which exploded myths about his people. Blacks, and sanctified souls. That they weren't smart enough. That all they did was jump, shout, get happy, sweaty. That a "pie in the sky" summed up their Gospel, their lives. Combat stereotypes. He did that at Syracuse. His scholarship, demeanor, carriage. His vocabulary, enunciation. Making white students go back to *their* dictionaries to check the words he utilized in class. Shocking those who talked with, came close to him, when they discovered his background, something they didn't understand. The blackness, the holyrolling, being "sanctified." And an *attorney?* The combination didn't click. . . . The combination for Nancy was the two of them. Even if he could never give her all of him. Because he wasn't doing with his life what he was supposed to. Instead of being assistant director of maintenance for the Buffalo City Schools, a good job, he'd be an attorney. And on weekends he'd travel, preach. Blend two worlds, the sacred with the profane. Marrying Nan did that for him. Loving her, all his taboos were broken. Bad became good. He became her "baby." He loved when she called him that, when she smiled during a shared laugh and called him "baby." Her "baby," said so naturally, as only a black woman could. "Baby"—said in the course of time—minutes, days, months, it became fact. He became baby for her and, like one, surrendered to her. Sucked her. Licked, fondled, with the exploration of an infant, every inch of her delicate brown skin. Skin he loved to kiss, lick, like a child's treat which must last long even as it must be enjoyed.

* * * * *

Two things that Stan enjoyed most about jogging were the way that it cleared his mind and the freedom. When he jogged, he thought more clearly than at any other time. Sheila once observed, "Too bad you can't strap on a typewriter and a desk when you run, like how African women carry their babies strapped to their breasts." When he jogged, stories, letters, songs, and poems, came, like now. A poem for Leah—picking up his pace, he recited the lines. The other thing about running, as opposed to driving through the city, was the freedom. He could go anywhere. No such obstacles as one-way streets or traffic congestion. If the sidewalks were full, he could weave between people, like a halfback in a tight game; or he could take to the grass or the street. Alleys, buildings, parks—shortcuts and detours—were all part of his course. Running through the streets was unlike competing on a track where distance, direction and goal weren't his decisions, where someone else compelled him to race. At the gun's sound, *this distance*, fast, faster than the others, his peers, colleagues who weren't his colleagues when they ran on the track, when he must beat them, even if he loved them, like Max, like "four de hard way." On the street, he "competed" with everyone and everything—walkers, joggers, buses, dogs, black Ford Mustangs, babies being wheeled in carriages, or a predicted snowfall before he reached his goal. Yet, on the street, he competed with no one because all were his peers. He passed them eye to eye, became acquainted with them; the anonymous houses he drove by became homes, havens, with identifiable inhabitants and traits when he ran, ... On a day like this one, he could run forever, ... The weather forecasters predicted snow tonight. In Buffalo, beginning around now, early November, you could predict *that* nightly for five months and have a high probability of correctness. He was at the corner of Delavan and Main Streets. From here, he could head home any number of ways, had run each of several routes for years, whether beginning at home, U.B., or a friend's place. Like a postman, he knew the names and habits of the dogs on these damned streets. If he took Main he'd run in the direction of Dia's, Delaware Park, the zoo, and U.B. It was the route he ran most. Delavan, which was the largest artery crossing his own street, would be the quickest, most direct route home. Or he could travel on Jefferson Street, the least direct route home, requiring that he take it and then zig-zag through a number of avenues. Jefferson was the most colorful way to go. It was, had always been, the central street of black Buffalo. The "funkiest" street in the Funky Nickel. Walk down Jefferson, or ride slowly, and you could read black Buffalo's social calendar. Telephone poles, trees, and boarded-up buildings held signs, placards, proclaiming big fun. Johnny Taylor at this joint. The Temptations at that club. James Brown at the Aud. The Mighty Clouds of Joy at Second Baptist. Shirley Caesar and James Cleveland at Kleinhains Music Hall. A tradition of advertising used by his people and white kids on college campuses. Jefferson, starting place and focal point of his community's one riot. In the 70's, "June 1st, whitey!" was the cry. But the prophecy promised more than the event. What event? There was no riot. The street, like Buffalo, like his people here, offered more than was delivered. Jefferson, lined by bars, liquor stores, churches. Taking it, he'd have to pass his father's church. Most of the "better," more refined black churches had moved away, towards the suburbs. They stayed, he had to hand that to them. He laughed and began trotting toward Jefferson.

* * * * *

Why did she stay so long with him? Was it love? Or was it, like with him, the church, not *believing* in divorce, in leaving? No. Because Rich disappointed her numerous times; he broke Stan's heart and she *had* left him. And moved closer to their son, her son. If their marriage was going to be saved, "revived," it would have to be today. "The time is now," James Cleveland sang in the gospel song. Were they singing that now in Rich's church, her church? "The time is now," or never. Like when Stan returned to L.A. that last time, against her advice, to simply "leave the b—— alone." Her advice, that "it was *never* going to work." He brought Sheila to Buffalo the summer before their wedding.

"Mom, Sheila. Sheila, this the lady who made me what I am."

"So now," Sheila said with a joking smile, "I know who's at fault." Nancy was babysitting for a neighbor and, later that day, sent the child out to Stan and Sheila, who sat in the yard, resting from their flight. She called from her bedroom window, "Stan, I'm sending Spike down with a letter and a newspaper clipping from Max. The clipping's about Maxi. She just won the Miss Nassau contest. I always thought she was something special."

And later, after the marriage, which she, but not Rich, attended, nor had any of his running buddies except for Alton, because it was arranged so quick, too quick, they talked over the phone. "I'm sorry your marriage isn't working out, son, but you and that girl weren't a good match. I never said anything, but now it's coming out."

"You never liked her anyway," his voice long-distanced and weak.

"It wasn't for me to like her. I wasn't going to have to live with her." She cleared her throat. "I don't want to run up your phone bill, but now that you've mentioned it, I have something to say. She always acted like she was doing you a favor by being with you. And *no girl*, I don't care if her family owns all of Omaha, is doing my son a favor by marrying him. I don't care if she is producing and whatnot. She's no better than us."

"Sheila's just quiet, mom, shy," his voice seemed to be dying out, getting even weaker.

"Okay, son, you just do what you think is right. She is a nice, polished young lady from a good family. I just don't want my child to be hurt. You've already been through enough, with your injury." She paused, clearing her throat again. "I'm glad you're out of school and working and all, but I'm sorry your relay team had to break up. I was in your room yesterday, looking at those track pictures. You-all were so good together, so free with each other. Why don't you call Max or one of the guys, talk with them? . . . I just don't want you to be hurt anymore than you have to be, you know? And I never said I didn't like her, I just didn't want you to . . . ."

"Be in a marriage like yours," he interrupted, his voice for a moment louder, clearer. . . .

She rose. She picked up her phone, the same phone she and Stan talked on back then. She called the church with a message. "This is Nancy Thompson. Tell my husband to meet *his family* at BB's this afternoon."

* * * * *

Sitting in the front pew during service, awaiting his turn to stand up in front and, as head deacon, expedite the morning's offering, Rich visualized the birth of his son like it was painted on the wall in front of him. He loved his son—with the love of a father. A father's love. Not the stuff of analogies, like mother's love: hugs, kisses, and petting when one is in pain. Fathers aren't thought of like that. And then, there's the mother's pain. Nine months and one day, or night, of pain. But he loved his son. Had always. No, he didn't carry, feel him inside. Nor did he have to eat, sleep, move differently because of him. But he'd loved him, from day one in the delivery room.

Theirs was an enlightened physician, Dr. Hernandez, who believed, "Bonding begins at birth. The first hands that hold the baby should be yours, Mr. Thompson. Yours, not mine." And they were. Rich remembered it well. The white and stainless room. Her cursing and crying "Jesus." "Jesus!" And when the baby was born—bloody, more stained and bloody than he could have imagined, he feared holding it. Hernandez positioned him at the foot of the table: "All you have to do is catch the baby, Mr. Thompson. It's coming." This said between intermittent cries from Nancy, "Ohhhhhh—Ohhhhh—Riiiiichhhh!" She was breathing correctly, or struggling to, but he couldn't hold her hand or stand by her side. He wanted to see her face yet couldn't. Could, if he left this position, but he was supposed to catch the kid. "The first hands that touch the baby . . . " The white spotlight beamed bright-hot on his sweating, straining, wife, Hernandez, and the nurse, while he waited in shadow at the foot of the delivery table.

"Ready Mr. Thompson?" Hernandez spoke to him while he focused on Nancy. "OK, now, Mrs. T, push. Pppush, puuush, puuush. Great. Now, one more big one . . . .

"Ohhhhhh, Jeesus, yyyes. Ohhhhh. Ohhhhhh. Oooohhhhhh." Her loud sounds drowned out Hernandez's soft tones. Richard waited, his hands ready.

"Ohhhhhh. Aaaahhhh. Ohhhhhhh. Ohhhhhhhh."

Her pain. She was working. Yes, the doctor was there, and the nurse. And he stood there, just waiting in a white robe at her feet, while his wife worked hard. Her every movement, murmur, moan, seemed loud, life-filled, death-filled. Hernandez uttered whispers—to himself, to the nurse? Rich couldn't discern his words over Nancy's cries. It was hours since she began labor. It must be true what they said about a woman passing death during childbirth. "Aaaaahhh. Aaaaahhhh. Aaaaaaaaah."

"It's coming, Mr. Thompson, it's coming." Hernandez instructed him to be ready for the baby. "OOOhhhh—OOOOhhh—OOOAAAhhhh." She was working, and it was coming out. Life, coming toward him. His child. Hers. She was working, finishing her task. Rich saw more of the child, held more of its body as it was squeezed out. He wished he could trade places with her, if just for a moment, and feel this life coming out, emerging, even as it was felt inside. He wished could help ease her pain, her "passing by death," but he also wondered how she felt now that it was over. With Hernandez by his side, he received into his cupped, trembling hands their baby boy, bloody and grayish brown and long. The pointy-headed infant was so tiny, squinting up at Rich, its eyelids barely open. He gently squeezed his son, feeling the tenderness through his rubber gloves. Closing his eyes for a moment, to halt the tears threatening to stream down his face, Rich silently thanked God, Nancy, and everyone present. Cradling the babe in his arms, he stood at the foot of the table and dared not move because there was a cord tying the child to Nancy. He remained perfectly still, waiting for Hernandez to come cut the cord. It must be cut, in order for him to move with his son. It needed to be cut, for the task to be complete. After holding the newborn for a precious few seconds, Rich surrendered him to Hernandez. Once the physician severed the umbilical cord, the child was washed, robed in white, and passed to her outstretched hands. They were wheeled out by the nurse. Rich followed. Hernandez patted his shoulder. "Sometimes the scissors snip right through the umbilical. This one was tougher. The first hands that held him were yours, Mr. Thompson. You'll remember this. And so will he, in his own way."

* * * * *

Stan wasn't going to run fast, break a sweat. Was going to trot down Jefferson leisurely, like this was a victory lap. Didn't know how many times he ran such laps, fifty, sixty, seventy? Couldn't recall one where he did so alone, but only those with the others, "four de hard way," dancing, jumping, slapping fives. Himself, Max, Ton, KK. The first time KK drove down this street, Jefferson, he compared it with his home, said there were similar streets in Accra. KK—the local press had a field day with the irony of his nickname because it brought to mind the white supremacist organization. They loved quizzing him about it. . . .

The rest of the track team were absent from the locker room. It was often this way. Max and KK were always the last ones on the track for practice; the four of them, the last ones off. The paint was peeling from portions of the locker room's white walls. The ceramic tile floor was a dingy yellow which would never be white again. From the ceiling, light fixtures hung every several yards. Thus, there were patches of darkness and light throughout the room. It was a team joke that wherever there was a puddle of water from the shower, it was dark. Team lockers were assigned alphabetically, making Stan and Alton neighbors, while Max's and KK's lockers were just two apart. An aisle separated the pairs. The four of them practiced later than the rest, wanting to get their baton exchanges smoother, faster. KK entered as his three friends, having already showered, dressed into their street clothes. He remained on the track to answer the questions of a local sports reporter. He jogged in barefooted, stripping off clothes and throwing them at his locker. "Max, man, I ain't got no new names for them damn white reporters. You give dem one, OK? I'm tired of da shit they ask me. They always wanna talk about the nicknames, or my adjustment to this here fuckin' place. Shit, man, I'm tired of dat. So next time, you talk wid them. You the one wid all de names." He plopped down on the bench in front of his locker, picked up his clothes. "Or you, Ton, or you, Son. I ain't doing no more damn interviews as long as I'm in this motherfuckin' country. No more." By now, his locker was open and he pitched out toiletries, tossing them hurriedly into his towel. "What the hell did this one ask, man?" Alton shouted across the room. "Yeah, mon, we all been asked some dumb ass shit, even the two Americans," Max chimed in. KK continued, "Yeah, he ask de same old simple shit, bout nick-names, relay records, and how different we all are to run so well together. Same ol shit." KK stood, towel draped across his shoulder, ready to hit the shower. His arm held the door of his locker. "Then that asshole started asking me shit y'all ain't never had to answer, none of y'all, not even Max. Motherfucker talk like Africa on another planet, intimating I ain't never *seen* whites or fuckin' television till I came ova here. But I ended the interview, decided to get dis white mother outa my face fast and to stop any more of em like him from comin' my way. You can have dat newspaper publicity shit, Max. It don't make you run faster." He slammed shut his locker. "I told him, Max, man, I use voodoo, on anybody and everybody, except y'all." Stan and Alton moved across the aisle, closer to the others. "Said I was giving him an interview only cause I wanted him to warn de other newspeople. Said I didn't give interviews back home 'cause he was right, in my village we don't have no papers, no radio or TV. And the next newsreporter come up to me asking about that KKK shit, I'm gonna put a curse on. Cause I don't believe in that media shit, and I agree with the KKK's anyway. Keep the damn races separate. The newsguy, he stopped smiling when I say all this. Stopped writin' on his pad and just begin lookin' at me, backin' up a little. I told him I was gonna use voodoo to *kill* me a reporter or two, next ones ask me anything about KKK's or my country." KK paused, grinning, "Asshole turn to leave by this time, but I grab his arm and hold it till I'm finished. I asked that scared motherfucker, `you heard how down in Haiti dey can kill ya, but you not really dead?' `Yeah,' he said. `Well, where the hell you think that come from? Africa,' I said. `Africa. My grandfather possessed the secret and showed me how. And I'm gonna perform it on you or another reporter if y'all don leave me the hell alone and let me run in peace.'" KK snapped his towel from around his waist, popped it in the air, and then swung it around his head in a wide, fast circle. "'Way-so-may!' That fool run like you, Son, when I let go his arm."

Stan paused at the intersection of Jefferson and Ferry. It stayed busy. The greasy aroma of a barbecue joint filled the air while the jingle-jangle of tambourines blasted from lines of cars waiting to use the only filling station for blocks around. A young clerk in soiled overalls dispensed gas and change, shuttling back and forth from the station to the next hungry vehicle. No self-service here. Inside the station was a group of men, four, five, six sitting around a counter, playing cards, seemingly oblivious to a job needing help. Across from this busy corner was a more common sight on Jefferson, a boarded-up building, a deserted filling station around which several men huddled. They huddled not because of the weather, but because of the liquid treasure inside the brown paper bag they passed around. Inside the bag was a bottle from which each took a long swig, holding it high, as though the tiny bottle were bottomless. Or, as though it were empty, and they each awaited the last drop. Not far away, a gun discharged. From another corner, a jazzy tune could be heard, ever so faintly. Somebody—Jimmy Smith or Buffalo's own Lucky Peterson?—was working out on an organ. Stan couldn't walk, run, or even drive down this street without feeling more alive. He loved running down Jefferson. Nowadays, his mom would say, "that's the only way to go down Jefferson, run down it, or drive fast, with your doors locked." He laughed. He loved this street; as Kojo said, "there's something makes you wanna move." Quickens you, makes you more alive, even as it surrounds you with threats of death. Death. Did KK really know how to make one a zombie, seem dead? They never discussed the subject after that day in the locker room. The light changed; trotting across Jefferson, Stan *vowed* to find KK.

* * * * *

She looked happy, smiling, holding the baby, in the photos he snapped of them. But it wasn't an easy delivery. Later, he would learn, they would learn, she couldn't give birth again. "He's so pretty, Rich. Looks like both of us. Look at those big hands, feet. His hair. It's so black and straight. If you look at his ears you can see what color he's going to be once he starts getting darker."

Babies have their own ways. As Gwen said, "They come out when they're ready, and they do most everything else that way, too." Stanford, named after Nancy's father, was so independent. When fed, he tried to feed himself, even before he could grasp. When read to, he attempted to snatch the book and make sounds along with the reader. "Dan dee" is what, at two and three, the baby called him, not "daddy," but "dan dee," unable to pronounce it better. Dan dee was the brand name of a potato chip manufactured and sold in Buffalo. For about a year, Rich brought home every Friday a small bag of Dan dee chips and a bottle of birch beer for the child. "'Dan dee,' the potato chip poppa," Nancy called him. Gwen, too, had a saying, "'dan dee's' bebop baby," Rich and Stan's weekly ritual. Upon entering the house, Rich yelled "Baby! Babyyy! Babyyyy!"—and the little one squealed with delight and crawled or toddled toward the sound. "Dan dee chips" was the child's reply to his dad's yell. Once they were in the same room, Rich tossed the bag to the baby who couldn't catch, but invariably tried, arms outstretched and fingers grasping air. "Hey, babyyy, you'll get it next time," was always Rich's response to the failed catch. He then rolled the bottle of birch beer across the brown-carpeted living room so that it softly hit a wall, and its impact sent Stan, bag of chips in hand, scampering after the bottle of soda. When the bottle came to rest, near the wall or floor lamp or coffee table, it, too, was retrieved by the baby, and both were taken to "dan dee" to open. But "dan dee, the potato chip poppa," faded with the passage of time; and "daddy's bebop baby," like an old record, played out, while Nancy weaved old and new worlds for their son with stories, stories Rich listened to, to hear what she said, and then turned away from. Her stories for the boy seemed of another world, an unreal world inhabited by just the two of them. Eventually, Stan became "the boy" when he discussed Stan with her. At times, Rich wished he were insistent about things concerning the child, whether it was naming their son after him, giving him a "little Rich," or a "Jr"; or whether it was simply that she back off at times, and cease being mom with such vengeance, so he could begin to be dad. Eventually, he gave up, but there were times when he wished to steal his son from her.

* * * * *

Running down Ferry toward home, Stan remembered what Mr. Guzza, his high school track coach, said about Buffalo, Western New York, during the fall. It was beautiful. Orange, fuchsia, red leaves hung on the trees. Most, however, were on the ground in multicolored piles which invited a plunge. The weatherman said snow tonight or tomorrow, but this felt like Indian Summer, not November. He was close to home now, near the old Twin Fair discount store parking lot, where they played football, tackle even though it was cement, against other neighborhood "gangs." Gangs. They weren't really that, he, Nut, Bubs, Donnie, Johnny Boy and, sometimes, Crazy Clyde. The Cambridge Boys, called that because three of them, Bubs, Donnie, and Clyde lived on that street. And it was on that street where they first began hanging together. "Hanging"—an apt word to describe their activities. Between football, hoops, and tales, mostly untrue, of exploits with girls, they did just that, "hung together." As Gwen said, they "tried to figure out what to do with themselves." "Always," he thought as he ran past the factory where he and Clyde once jumped the fence because Clyde pulled the fire alarm on the corner and red dye stained his hand. They leapt right into the spot where the factory's guard dog was; Stan was almost bitten as he scaled the barbed wire fence, ripping his jeans, barely escaping the leaping, snarling German Shepard. Crazy Clyde. Where was he now? Working in a factory, married? Left town, dead, in jail? Like with so many of his old friends, Stan didn't know; the gang split up after Johnny's death, during high school. After high school, during college, Stan stopped hanging with them altogether, except for an occasional call or chance run-in. Now he was near Carl Street, Patty D's house, where he hid, trying to crawl under her sister's bed. Her grandmother wasn't supposed to have been home yet, and he couldn't fit under the bed. Her grandmother called his mom, told. Told what? They hadn't done "the do." Almost, kissing and grinding, sweating and feeling one another. Running down Carl Street, he increased his pace. He was almost home. Carl, where the other neighborhood gang hung. Terry and Sticks and Monk-man and Monk's brothers. How many brothers? Eight, spanning twelve, fifteen years, so that Carl Street always had enough fellas to challenge, play, or fight them. But they never fought, except for on a court, field, or track. Turning the corner at Carl, he began sprinting. It felt good, running, remembering. . . . He raced his father. At eleven, twelve, he was a member of the Urban League's Boy Scout troop. The troop boxed with gloves, wrestled on mats, sprinted on UB's track. The first time he ran on a real track, he beat every boy in the troop. He came home childishly proud, proclaiming at the dinner table, "I'm the best runner in the troop. Can beat a whole lot of people." The voice directly across the table warned, "*Don't brag.*"

"I'm not bragging. It's true. I beat the whole troop."

"Bragging will get you in trouble; there's always somebody better than you."

"I can beat you."

There was a point to be made, and they made it in the middle of the street, directly following dinner. They raced at the distance of perhaps one hundred yards, from the corner of the block to the beginning of their house. The winner, the first one to cross the pillar of their porch. How did they decide on the distance? It was clear that they must run toward home. Stan knew his mom feigned disinterest during dinner but watched from the upstairs bedroom window. That guest room, later, after their split, became his father's. Nancy stood in the room and pulled back the white curtain just enough, so that from the street, you probably wouldn't notice her, unless you knew to glance up for her, spying on them as they walked together toward the starting point, a telephone pole's shadow in the street. But there was too much distance between them, and neither spoke a word to the other. Out playing, other kids paused, and quizzed, "Stan, where you goin' with your dad?" "Nowhere, just to the corner pole, to race him." *Him*, said intentionally by Stan, a reflection of their real distance, a gulf he hoped would be reflected at the race's end by how far he left *him* behind. Their walk reminded Stan of the gunfighters in his favorite cowboy shows, *Gunsmoke, Bonanza*, dealing with their differences out in the street, so everyone can see.

Everyone seemed out that summer evening, adults sitting on their porches, reading, rocking, watching the kids in the street. Boys playing touch football, the "Bills" against the "Jets," some black kid wanting to be Joe Namath, because of his white shoes and winning ways. In the opposite direction, toward the middle of the block, a group of girls, Nettie, Selena, and company danced in the street. Still too young for clubs or anything other than chaperoned parties, the girls danced like their entry into womanhood depended upon it. In their own eyes, they were no longer too young. The hand movements they used doing "Mary Mack"; the roll of the hips that held up their hula hoops; the steps and jumps of hopscotch were incorporated into their dance moves. Their lithe brown bodies, hinting of enticements to come, showed off and embellished what they saw on the last episode of *"Soul Train."* But as the girls saw the pair, son and father, walking down the middle of the street toward the corner; as they heard someone say, "Stan's gonna race his father—gonna smoke em!"—they turned to watch. Which of them issued the challenge? His father wanted to teach him a lesson. *Don't brag.* But he hadn't. Who decided on the starting line? One of the porch-sitting adults? Mr. Buck, of the smelly cigars and story after story of Jackie R. and the Brooklyn Dodgers? Or Miss Perry, snuff-dipper and wild spitter, whose front yard testified? Who yelled "get on your mark"? One of Stan's friends? Nut? Or Clyde, who, it was rumored, was in prison somewhere—Attica, Elmira? Or Nettie? Once fine Nettie, with a body at fourteen that made her street dance, her walk, the object of stares from men as well as boys. Which of their neighbors lining the street bellowed some of his father's past athletic exploits, how he could always out think and outrun his opponents? Who, as they stood behind the telephone pole shadow which was their starting line, yelled, "get set!"? Was it now-dead Johnny Boy? Or his dad, Johnny, Sr.? At the time, the Davises lived in a red brick house directly across from their own. It wasn't until after Johnny's death that Mrs. Davis departed and Johnny, Sr. took up residence above BB's. Stan didn't remember. He didn't think either Davis uttered a word until the race began, with each cheering his peer. No, the call, the yell, the cry, originated from up the block, in the vicinity of their house. Then, standing beside one another at that shadow, was the first time Stan heard someone remark about their resemblance. Mrs. Morris shrieked, "Rich, that boy's 'bout big as you. Look just like you, too!" Those words compelled Stan to wish even harder to beat his father, to erase any resemblance with speed. But he did favor him. They both wore green. He, the faded green of his scouting uniform. His father, olive green linen slacks with a light green dress shirt; he'd discarded his tie, but kept on his brown leather dress shoes. Stan'd changed to his sneakers. "Go!"—did one person shout it? It seemed chorused by the whole block, both sides of the street. "Go!" Like the girls in the street sang it at the end of one of their dance tunes. "Go!" The boys taking a break from football and the porch-sitting elders used it to test their comparative loudness. "Go!" It seemed that the sound emanated from his house as well. He remembered the call as though it was uttered not once, but a thousand times. "Go!" He burst from behind the shadow like an unleashed dog. Burst, scrambling out, falling on all fours, but using his hands to break his fall and propel himself forward. His desperate dash must have surprised his father who was left, smoked. Who didn't give up, stop running, but was simply left in the dust. It was evident, as they ran, that his father was faster than he, as his father's long strides gained on his shorter ones as they approached the finish. But the man couldn't overtake him because he'd been left too quickly at the line by his scrambling son whose race was complete when he looked up at their house, and saw a slight closing of white curtains in the guest bedroom. Stan streaked past the pillars of their house and continued on, another twenty yards, showing what he had left to Nettie and the girls who were already reforming their line, preparing to practice more steps. . . .

* * * * *

Nancy showered quickly, rubbing the soap over their sweat, washing away all traces of their lovemaking. She wanted to leave the house before Stan possibly returned. She'd walk to BB's. Johnny or one of the regulars would pick her up, but she needed the walk. She called John to reserve a place for them.

"Johnny, set my table special for me today."

"Nancy, I always sets it special for you on Sundays."

"This Sunday, John, my family's going to join me."

"The Preach and Stan, too?"

"Yeah, John."

Today, either they'd become a family again, or she'd burn down the house or kick them both out or just keep on walking. She scribbled a note for Stan and taped it to his door. She believed they'd come, but it would be her job to keep them there.

* * * * *

Stan was now on his own block, coming from the same direction as in the race with his father. He took to the middle of the street, sprinting toward home as though the years hadn't passed and the houses weren't inhabited by different folk. Disregarding cars, he raced down his street as though his old friends weren't imprisoned, long gone, just "making it," or dead. No, as he ran, as he stretched out toward home, they were *there*, alive, young—Johnny, Nettie, Nut, lining the street; and he, hearing their cheers, looked up at his mom, having outraced his father, beaten him.

He used the spare key kept under the mailbox in a magnetized case. Once inside, he entered his bedroom, which also faced the street. Prior to entering, he read a note from his mom to meet her at BB's; snatching it off the door, he crumpled and threw it to the floor. "Naw, mom." With black curtains and shades, selected during his teens, his was the darkest room in the house. The white walls held black-framed pictures of black athletes and musicians, collected during his college career. "Col-

lected" wasn't really the right word, as some were gifts. A couple
had been small, wallet-sized photos which were blown up. Sam
Cooke and Marvin Gaye sang to him and one another from op-
posing walls. Trane and Billie flanked the head of his bed on either side. An African mask, a gift from KK, hung between them,
directly over the bed. And the wall facing the bed held three pictures of athletes—Jesse Owens at the Berlin Olympics; John
Carlos and Tommie Smith, heads bowed, black-gloved hands
held high in protest; and, finally, a shot of `four de hard way,'
trotting around the track together at practice. It was a shot
which was once included in the school's admissions brochure.
They each received a complementary photo. Although there was
little space on his walls for additional pictures, there were two
more he wanted—Dinah Washington, for his mom, and Hassan.
Next to his bed, on one side, sat a tall dresser/desk. His matching nightstand held a table lamp, the shade of which was angled
to shed more light on the bed. Stan retrieved his journal, began
writing in it, first the poem for Leah.

> *You tried. But I'm a poet,*
> *You could never be a poet's woman.*
> *For she should bring sadness*
> *like waiting.*
>
> *Saturdays and Summers*
> *should be sinless and mute.*
> *Couldn't you have kept the pattern?*
>
> *With the others—*
> *basketball in some gym,*
> *working on my left.*
> *Frequenting frequented spots,*
> *alone . . . .*

But then, he couldn't recall any more; one of his father's favorite scriptures kept getting in the way. He wasn't sure why. When had it first come to him today? "Even the youths shall faint and be weary, and young men shall faint; but they that wait upon the Lord shall renew their strength, they shall run and not be weary, they shall walk and not faint." His father's church, were they out yet? Where was his mom? Then, he remembered Smythe's sermon. "Too little." Every man was, yet every man's situation was significant to that man or woman. Like Leah. He never saw her so angry. He examined the knife wound on his left arm. It would eventually heal and become just another scar. Too bad that wouldn't just happen with his cancer. Too bad things didn't work out like Dr. Goldstein said, "We've learned how to keep the disease at bay for months, and sometimes even to produce remissions that last for years." Goldstein put his arm around Stan, continuing, "You're an old track man. Well, with this disease, we're not running a sprint, but a marathon. What's most important, Stan, is not how fast we run the first few miles, but when we break the tape." Now, Doc. Goldstein didn't even know where he was. After being told of the cancer's return, he just left, but he still took his medicine, what was left of it, periodically. Eventually, he'd send Leah the poem. There were seven posters on his wall. Five of the people in them were dead. According to Ton, he needed seven people to find KK. With seven, could he locate Sheila? And do what, and say what? He reached for his phone, dialed information in Chicago. The operator found no number for KK. He turned on his tape player, put in his Hassan tape. Listened to "To Inscribe," which, being the last cut on the album, was recorded five times on this tape, so he could listen to it again and again. Full chords, arpeggios, Hassan stacking notes upon notes. He didn't know what happened to Hassan. His father never finished telling him. He shut off the tape player, rose from his bed, went into his father's room. His father's old service footlocker. Kneeled at it. Its padlock wasn't closed. He rummaged through it till he found his father's service revolver and, underneath it, some shells. He took them out, closing the locker. Went back to his bedroom, to doze for a few. Thought of the prayer his mom, or father?, taught him to say before bed. "Now I lay me down to sleep. I pray the Lord my soul to keep. If I should die before I wake, I pray the Lord my soul to take." As a child, he practiced saying it rapidly, to get into bed more quickly each night. Not that he desired to go to bed earlier; it was merely the challenge of reciting it faster and flawlessly. He frequently recalled that prayer before he went to bed. Rising, he stripped off his clothes, then loaded the gun, putting all six shells in it and placing it on his nightstand. Once in bed, he turned the tape on again; there were probably two more recordings of "To Inscribe" on it. Then, covering his head with his pillow, he closed his eyes.

* * * * *

Dia's four favorite authors were Dickinson, Dostoyevsky, Hughes, and Hurston. She bought and read everything she could by them. Even when she was reading someone else, she also read a work by one of them. She reserved seasons for reading each of the four. Dickinson and Dostoyevsky, because they focused on the hidden life and hibernation, were particularly suited to autumnal reading, when the earth itself changed for the winter. Hughes, especially his poetry and Simple stories, was ideal for the rhymes and rhythms of summer. Hurston's time was during the holidays. If she read anything lengthy during the Thanksgiving or Christmas seasons, it was her lady, Zora. Today, she began *Their Eyes Were Watching God*. She couldn't say the number of times she'd read it. "I keep coming back to it like it's a lollipop or medicine." She started reading this morning, after finishing her Sunday papers, The *Buffalo Courier Express* and The *New York Times*. She read through the local paper and skimmed sections of The *Times*, reading it was a week-long endeavor. But she closed Hurston's novel after reading the first three paragraphs. She loved the novel's opening, knew the words verbatim. Wished she'd read this book as a child so she could have recited these paragraphs in one of those school speech contests held for youngsters. But the lyricism of the opening passage wasn't why she closed the book.

"So the beginning of this was a woman, and she had come back from burying the dead." She scribbled Stan a note: "I can't be with you any longer. Women don't like coming back from burying their dead. I guess I'm burying the living. Claudia." She grabbed her coat and keys to go to the phone booth. She was going to call him to ask that he come over.

* * * * *

Her call awoke him. An uncustomary urgency, "I need you to come over now." He told her she'd have to pick him up. That would give him time to shower and get ready. It took about fifteen minutes to get from her place to his. He planned to see her later today, anyway. He bought her a little stuffed lion during his dinner break on Thursday. It was a long day for him, nine a.m. to nine p.m., as Steve was out of town. It was cute, caramel-colored with a bright red ribbon for a bow-tie. As he dried off, the phone rang. He ignored it. In a few minutes, Dia would be outside, blowing her horn. He dressed quickly. His gym bag stayed packed with running equipment and toiletries. Into it he also stuffed his journal, underwear, jeans, and a sweater. That left just enough room to put the toy lion in atop the clothing and the Hassan tape and his father's gun in the bag's side pocket. He was descending the stairs, bag over his shoulder, as she drove up.

"Hi." As he leaned over to kiss her mouth, Dia offered her cheek.

"Where's your car?"

Stan said nothing, but instead turned his attention to the window. The radio was playing a frenetic gospel tune. She sped toward the expressway. This wasn't the way you normally went to her place; it was his route to work, downtown. But on Sundays the expressway was nearly empty and therefore fast. The sound and the speed compelled him to say *something*, make small talk, or get to the point and ask what was up.

"Here, Stan, take these." She pulled out from beneath her seat two white envelopes. "Give these to your mom and Leah." She pulled out a third which she had sat on. "This one's for you. Read it now?"

He opened his envelope and read its contents. Then, he gave his attention back to the window, the sky. It was overcast. A jet, its white tail streaking the grayish-blue, sped away, higher, westward. "My car's over Leah's house."

She turned up the radio's volume. The guitars were twanging, the organ screeching, the drums pounding, pounding. There was clapping. But he couldn't understand a word. He reached over, turned off the radio. She turned it back on, pushing in "The Dia Tape," Donny Hathaway singing "Someday We'll All Be Free." He talked, as much to the desolate city streets they whizzed by as to her. "Before Gwen went out to L.A. one time, she took me shopping. It just so happened that she was leaving on my birthday, so she took me downtown, to Woolworth's and said I could have anything I wanted. Anything in the store. She had money for her trip and then some. The band sent it to her. We must have spent forty-five minutes walking up and down the aisles. Trains, bikes, electric racing car sets, all the things I wanted. And you know what I picked out? A Zorro outfit. I was crazy about Zorro. Couldn't have cost more than six dollars. A black cardboard mask, a plastic pointer which held the chalk, a box of chalk, and a silly plastic cape. That's what I picked out. To this day," he turned from the window to her, "I've never again been given the opportunity to chose whatever I wanted, and know I was going to get it." He rolled down his window. Cold, crisp air hit his face. "Yeah, that decision was hard to make. They all are." He picked up his gym bag, opened it, took out the stuffed animal, put in the envelopes. "That's for you, hon." He placed the lion on the seat. He leaned over and kissed her cheek.

"Thanks." She rubbed the toy against the spot he kissed.

"Hope you like it."

"I've always wanted a lion."

"What're you going to name him?"

She held it out. "How do you know it's a him? Oh, that's right. The `hims' have manes. How about Holden?"

"Doesn't sound lion-like to me."

"I like holding him, OK? What would you have me name him? Leo? I bet you'd like Leo. Leo the lion, Proudhammer. Nope, his name's Holden, and he doesn't have a surname."

"I wouldn't think he would. I'm not gonna ask where you come up with these names."

"That's cause you already know." She steered the car onto her street. They were almost there.

He did know, books and films. She lived in one of the city's oldest neighborhoods. The car rumbled over the cobblestone road sprinkled with leaves. Leaves, piled along the curb, lined the red brick street. On some lawns, the multi-colored leaves weren't raked and were scattered across the grass like spectators in a stadium for a meet. Two more blocks. He picked up his bag, held it in his lap, feeling his father's gun through the canvas.

Walking up the flights of stairs to her apartment, following her, he was certain she was the one. He leaned against the wall as she fished in her large, tan leather purse for her keys. It took awhile. If he was with anyone else, he'd still want to be with her. Not Leah, not Maxi, not even his long-lost Sheila. Dia. She kept her car and house keys separate. Carried all kinds of junk in the purse—books, notebook paper, pens, pencils, make-up, a small tape recorder. He wouldn't be surprised if she pulled out a pair of shoes. Finally, she found the key. After she opened the door and entered, he lingered in the hallway. A drab grey, it made him think of the stockroom at work. She went to the bathroom, the only other room in the apartment. He waited until he heard the bathroom door swing open the second time before entering.

"What were you doing out there?" She went over to her TV, turning it on, but without sound. Her stereo had already been on, at a low volume. Classical music flowed from the speakers.

"Nothing, Dia, just thinking. What's that playing?"

"I'm not sure. I'm trying to learn more about classical music, so I've been listening to this station." She knelt in front of the refrigerator. "I know you don't drink wine, but I've also got orange soda and apple juice."

"No thanks," he sat down on her bed, dropping his bag next to him.

Leaving the frig, she sat across from him, against a wall, using one of the floor pillows for her back.

"I can't accept what you say in your letter."

She was watching a black and white movie. He didn't know its title, couldn't identity the actors, but their faces looked familiar. "I know." She sipped from her glass.

The movie was from the forties, he guessed. Men in fedoras and double-breasted suits with wide lapels. "What happened?" Saying this, he brought his bag closer to him, leaning an elbow on it.

"You happened, Stan. You. You're not anything like . . ."

"You thought I'd be," he interrupted her.

She rose, went to the TV, turning up the volume so that it was just audible above the music. Then, she returned to the refrigerator. Getting a bottle of wine, she slammed the door. "No. You're not anything like you *want* to be, really." She brought a box of starch from the cupboard. "Want some?" She offered him the box.

"OK," he took it, pouring out a big white chunk which he broke in half. Half he put back in the box.

She rested against the wall. "Did you ever see a movie called `The Slender Thread,' starring Anne Bancroft and Sidney?"

He placed the box of starch on his bag. "No, I don't think so? Sidney who? Poitier?"

"Yes, dear, the only Sidney. It's about a suicide. I don't remember it all, but Bancroft takes pills to kill herself and calls this suicide hotline, where Sidney is answering the phone. There's a point when he talks about reaching through the phone and dragging her back. But then, Stan, there's a point when he just says `go ahead.' It's like she endures more minutes for him. I don't know, Stan. I don't know. I don't know. I don't know what to do with you. I know how you feel about me," she sipped her wine, continuing, "but it's not enough, not nearly enough. I can't even remember the rest of the movie, talking to you. I guess he saves her; I think he saves her. *He* thinks he's saved her, at least for awhile. But she never sees him. He remains invisible. All I can remember right now is that near the end he smiles that Sidney smile, that Oscar-winning smile. And then he chooses to leave her the hell alone." She finished her glass.

"Black man's burden. Save souls and remain invisible. Sounds like my father. Dia, our lives aren't books or movies, they're real."

"Some of them are real."

"Some of which, lives or books and movies?" He picked up the starch and unzipped the side pocket of his bag.

"Some of both, Stan-man, some of both. The trick is in the choosing. Like you said, decisions *are* difficult."

"But this isn't," he said, getting the gun out of his bag. He held it up. "This isn't."

"Go ahead. Do it, Stan," she rose and walked to the stereo, turning it up. "Do it." She yelled. "Do it. You're a religious man. And you've got your Sunday Sacrament, honey," she held up a broken piece of starch and her bottle of wine. "Take your communion and then do it. Pray to your father, and I don't mean God or Jesus; I mean Richard. Make sure you pray to him before you pull the trigger, 'cause he's the real reason you're doing this." She stopped, sighed "And, don't worry, 'cause you've got a witness. I'll even record it if you want me to. I just hope my batteries are good," she nodded at her purse by the bathroom door. "Isn't this what you wanted, the situation for a spectacular death? A death you'd probably be planning even if you weren't sick. You *are* sick. Maybe we should practice first, you know, with blanks, or I should borrow my dad's movie camera. Wanna wait till tomorrow so I can get it? Then we can practice and everything, so when I film it, it'll be right, a *real* spectacle . . . you know? . . . a sight for sore eyes. . . ." Her voice trailed off. Dia's head was down; she was sobbing.

Because of the TV and stereo, he yelled. "But I am sick! I didn't plan this! And I'm tired of fighting it."

"What about all the stories you told me about?—all those people who've beaten the disease?" She looked up. "You're beaten Stan. Beaten. You talk about killing yourself. You're already dead. You just forgot to lie down."

He felt that her words, as always, were the words of a book or a movie. Yet, this time, he couldn't dismiss them with ease. Instead, because of her words, he gripped the gun tightly in one hand and the piece of starch in the other. He dared not let either go, either drop. Either, he felt, would explode and, with the explosion, the room, he, and she would also perish. Perish. A word they used in church. Perish. It meant more than just dying. In his father's church, they sang, "I wouldn't mind dying, if dying was all." "My father," he began again, focusing on the white men on the screen as though they were his audience, "was, for such a long time, the best man I had ever seen." Then he stopped, went to the stereo, tv, knelt down and turned them off. Leaning on the tv, he remained on his knees, speaking up to her, choosing his words carefully, saying them softly and slowly, as though Dia *was* a newsreporter on an assignment and he didn't want to be misquoted. "Not the best *black* man, but the best man, period. I guess every kid feels this way. But even when I grew up and knew better, I still saw what a grand failure he was. Grand. With himself, my mom, me. And I decided," he paused, raising the pistol higher, "to never be like him. I decided, if he did one thing, I'd do the opposite."

"And so, since he is living, you wish to die," she said, wiping away tears.

"Or vice-versa."

CHAPTER
5
Is not Given

Turf. That church *might* be Rich's, but this bar, BB's, was definitely hers. Nancy entered, and black and gold-trimmed bar stools swirled; warm brown smiles turned to greet her. A chorus of greetings: "Nancy, girl. Where you been?" "Before you go to your seat, lady, come here give me a hug." "Hey Nan, you just the person I been wantin' to see." Several patrons left their tables to come to hers, and she, like a good politician gave a smile, a wink, a quick word to each. In the church, there are church mothers, older women whose blessing is just that, whose word is sage. Here, she was it. Johnny danced from behind the bar, "gimme mine, Nance." The tall, well dressed woman and the short, white-aproned man hugged, swaying to the booming bass of the speakers. Johnny's round face featured a glowing, jack-o-lantern smile which welcomed her; then, clasping her outstretched hand tightly in his, he said, "Nance, I'll come back later and take your order myself. When your mens arrive." Showing deep dimples, he smiled even wider, as though two of the departed black heroes were condescending from the wall to join her at the table. "Gotta get back to the bar." She held to his hand. "Johnny, let *me* handle the music today."

* * * * *

Stan didn't desire the radio on, the tape playing, but if he turned it off, she'd just switch it on again. Donny Hathaway was singing Nina Simone's "To be Young, Gifted and Black," the one song he was uncertain about taping. All the others were love songs. But she loved Simone, "for her music and her life," so he taped it. He'd do any damn thing for her. Screw his plans, he had none. There wasn't a whole lot he ever really finished. He was just like his neighborhood, so much damned promise, so little achieved. "When I Have Fears" was the poem she mentioned. Well he had fears, fears that he wasn't as young, anymore, or as gifted.

"Dia, I read somewhere that women who've undergone tubal ligations can have the process reversed. That's what I want you to do, so you can have our baby. I've never wanted anyone to have my child before, not even . . . ."

"Sheila. Look, I'm driving you home, dropping you off, and that's it, there's no more to say. I'll just start screaming again."

"You know I'm crazy about you, and . . . ."

"And," she interrupted, "*you* need to see someone, Stan, a shrink. You ever read Gwendolyn Brooks' poem, "the mother?" I wish I had my copy. The truth is, I've never wanted to go nine months for any man."

"This is a proposal. Marry me."

"You *are* crazy. I'm not the marrying kind. Go back to Leah. What about her son, you sure he's not your kid? I wish he was, 'cause then I'd of sent you back to her a long time ago, express mail."

She sighed. "You remind me of those interracial couples I see clutching on to one another. They're almost always holding hands or arms or waists, or whatever. You know, Stan, I simultaneously admire and pity them. Cause it seems that they're holding one another to say to the world, 'screw you, we love or like or need one another, and we're going to display it openly.' That's fine, but one has to deal with the fact that they can't go through life grasping somebody else's, anybody else's, hand, like your momma seems to have communicated. And artificial crutches, like holding hands all the time, in some weird show of love won't get it. I think you want me to show something to the world, to your parents, or your past. It's like you wish you could dig up old Max and show him. To say nothing of Sheila. You want to find her not because you still love her, but because you loathe her. That sister was good and tough, and knew it. You knew it, too, but weren't sure about yourself, in spite of your track medals and degree. And as soon as you both gained that knowledge, the shit was over, Stan, the marriage was over, you couldn't keep her. And now, you can't keep me. I'm gone. I'm dropping you off so you can find your momma or kill your daddy or whatever. I don't care. No, that's wrong, I do care. A part of me wishes we could have made it, wishes I *could* have our baby, to show the world that it did work, that we did work for awhile. But hell no, I'm not into outward signs of inward failures. I'm not into cowards who give up. Know what I mean? I'm not a trinket or a medal, and a baby, a child, sure the hell isn't." She cried as she stared at the wide, black road ahead.

"Dia, take me to BB's."

"Okay Stan."

Minnie Riperton was singing "Loving You," one of *their* songs, from one of the best days of his life. He resisted her words as she was uttering them, and now, as he pondered them. Didn't she love him? He resisted her words, thinking of Max's maxim, "don't fall in love, just love." Maybe that was what Dia did. He resisted her words, like when he was working out, bench pressing a new, heavier weight without a spotter. And he couldn't lift it, but couldn't drop it, either. There was a point when he simply resisted it, held it up, trusting the big-veined arms he inherited from his father. Resisted it, due to the strength in those arms from *his* workouts, *his* lifting. He fought her words and the thoughts they brought to mind—his father's words about black males perpetually being boys and black females always and forever old. As Minnie, sweet songstress, chirped like a sparrow, he fought and listened and looked. Ahead of them, the setting sun was a flaming reddish-orange. It looked gigantic, as if they could reach it in five, ten minutes, at most, like he could run the distance. He wanted Dia to drive it. Few people were out. Most were probably in, watching the Bills lose another one. Buffalo's team. His team. His father's. One of the few things they agreed upon. Live and die with the Bills. He chuckled. Sounded like someone who'd overspent for Christmas. Christmas. Would he still be alive then? The Bills wouldn't be. As Minnie Riperton sang, "Lovin' you is easy 'cause you're beautiful," he was reminded of her death by cancer, breast cancer. Then, he tried to think about something else, the lack of cars on the road, the news, the weather. He wanted Dia to steer this damned jalopy anywhere, in any direction, toward any destination but where she was headed. He wanted to scream above Minnie's sweet song and the hum of the motor, for Dia to drive 'til they ran out of gas; to head east, toward Albany, or take the expressway north to Canada, Toronto. Last August was the most recent time he visited there, for Caribana, the West Indian festival. He'd journeyed to meet Max, the spirit of Max, amidst the jumping, jangling and funny-time Caribbean accents. His two days there were special, shopping underground, eating conch out of the shell, partying. He loved Toronto. As a kid, he envisioned Canada as a haven for black people, that better place where racism was less. In part, this was due to the lore of black Buffalonians, many of whom discussed moving across the so-close border, spouting such lines as, "Man, you can get better clothes up in Toronto." "It's cleaner up there, man." Or, "there's not as much racism up in Canada. White folks treat you better up there." In part, Stan believed that the image of Canada was one of the rituals, a part of the heritage, of African Americans, handed down from slavery, his people's continual search for a border to be crossed where the burdens of blackness would ease, would cease. Right now, he wanted his carefully-driving Dia to chauffeur him anywhere, to Canada, the setting sun, or the moon, just so she wouldn't leave him. She *was* a careful driver. It was the only careful thing she did. Watching her, tight-lipped, grimly focused on the road, gripping the wheel with both hands, it appeared that he was a child whose safety was her job; she was dropping off her little one for his first day of school. Part of him wanted to tell her to take him to the hospital, to show her that he hadn't given up. Wouldn't if she stayed with him. She was right. He'd devise a plan for suicide even if he wasn't sick. Search for a "magic bullet" not to kill the cancer, or himself, but to put to death the life he was given. Maybe he just needed to accept it. They were now at BB's, and she put the car in park but kept the motor running.

"Later, Son," she said softly, turning, facing him. He stared at her as she held Holden close to her breast. "Later, Son," she revved the engine, to keep the car going or to rouse him, but it reminded him of those old gangster movies that she loved. She was the driver, and he, the hold-up man. It was her job to wait with the car running and to be ready when he would flee: ready, waiting for the sign, the gun shot. But Dia wouldn't drive to Canada, and she wouldn't wait for him. She was clutching Holden to her face; he thought he still detected tears. No, her tears *had* dried. She *had* stopped crying.

"Is it really just 'later,' Dia?"

"You know it's not. Goodbye, Stanford."

"Okay, Claudia." When he leaned over to kiss her, she didn't turn away, as he thought she might. She was perfectly still as he kissed her parted lips. He wanted to make love to her. He could arouse her, right here, right now. His lips moved down to her neck, while his hand stroked the inside of her thigh. His so-sensitive Dia, but for once, she didn't moan, didn't move. And when his hand touched, not her breast, but Holden, and he felt the tightness of her grip on the toy, he stopped, leaning back, and gently squeezing her right hand, which was cradled in his left. Turning away from her, he unlatched the door with his free hand, kicking it open with his foot. Retrieving his bag, he stared at her beautiful, tear-stained face and her breast, where she tightly clutched Holden; then, he released her hand as he exited the car because he would have pulled her with him if he hadn't let go. "Goodbye, Son," she said softly. He slammed the door firmly and walked away, not looking back.

* * * * *

She stared at her son the second he entered. Stared intently as he talked with Johnny, as Johnny directed Stan to her table, but he refused, and stood by the bar. The pockets of his olive army fatigue jacket bulged. She'd never been in them, but *knew* their contents because of the many times she watched him prepare for a workout. In the breast pockets, weightlifting gloves and gym pass. In the side pockets, lock and keys. He wore his black sweat outfit. Heavy cotton, so thick nothing else could fit in the washer with it. The sweat shirt, extra-extra large; the pants, large. Each of these contained pockets, too. He needed pockets, ever since his gangly, fast-growing adolescence of all legs, arms, and hands. He needed pockets *every*where for those hands, which were at times for him the worst of extremities. Like when he sang a solo as the Easter Bunny in the grammar school play or later when he was in college, being interviewed by a sports reporter, and his hands searched the air for the exact words, like a preacher, like his father. Pockets. Her son invariably carried something in them, his hands, for one. His hands were strong now, like all of his body, but to her they still seemed to seek shelter or task, something to hide in or hold.

From here, using the one-way window in the sound room behind the bar, she could see Stan, could see each person, the length of the bar, and the front door. She could scope the entire place, but no one could see her. It was a security measure Johnny added at her insistence, when they remodeled BB's. She knew the songs she was going to play. She was using this song to "warm up," like Stan would always do before a race. If Rich was late arriving, she would play more "warm-up" cuts, but she didn't think he would be.

She retreated to this tiny box of a room to try to save them through music, their one common love. She knew the songs to play. But it was essential, no matter what, that she remain in this box, with its one-way mirror, sound equipment controls, security switches and guns. Rich believed she babied Stan, so she must keep out of it, remain silent, except for the sounds she spun.

* * * * *

Entering the club, he glanced up at his photo, as always. "Stan!" Johnny hailed him from behind the bar. Bar stools swirled with the sound. Some smiled. Several of his old friends from the neighborhood were present. Snooks, Cobbs, and Donnie played pool in the rear. Candy and Nettie, dressed to kill, were seated near the pool table, talking, watching. Their short, tight dresses, black and red, respectively, revealed brown thighs which were crossed in the direction of the pool players. Other regulars were at the bar and around the room. The same ol' same ol' crowd. Looking pretty, looking good, looking happy for another weekend or day or night. Nettie waved as she noticed him. She had the shapeliest legs in high school. They still were nice. Heavier, but still whispering seductive secrets Stan felt she'd work hard to disclose. Since his return home, they kept a running joke about going out on a date, a joke revived from high school days, when she carried a crush on him, but thought him "too quiet and stuck up" to date. Candy waved and smiled his way. He followed suit. Ladies in waiting. Dresses too short, too tight. Shoes too cheap, heels too high. He couldn't see their feet, but knew what Nettie, one of his steady customers, was wearing. The red leather three-inch open-toe pumps. Last month, she purchased them and the red leather purse on her arm. He needed to stop looking their way. Cobbs gave him the power sign. He acknowledged it in like manner, but he wanted to run across the room and off Cobbs, hit him hard, such as when they played street football together and there was just one more blood between him and the goal. He wanted to grab Nettie, and dance with her, slow-drag with her out the door, holding her tight till he was hard and she was soft, so soft she'd follow his lead forever. He wanted to fire his gun into their table, their game, so they could begin to see past it, past this room, this bar, and their sorry-ass lives. Nettie was one of his oldest friends yet around who was not totally wasted, in jail, or dead. He wanted to rap to her, in rhythm with the music, till she sensed the urgency and death in this room; till she would take off her red dance shoes and flee with him, across the Peace Bridge to Canada, like runaway slaves to freedom.

"Heh, Johnny. You know what I want." Stan placed the shoulder bag at his feet. James Brown was singing, "This is a Man's World." An old classic, like every Sunday. "Thanks," he said as the o.j. was placed in front of him. "Where's my mom? She's usually here by now."

"She'll be back."

"So she was here?"

"Yeah, yeah, but you know her. She'll be back, 'pecially if she's expecting you."

"I know."

J.B. crooned, "This is a man's world." He wondered where his mom was. Where Dia was. He wanted her here, to slow drag with, to lose himself in the music and her embrace. "This is a man's world," James was begging, in his raspy, down-home voice, for somebody to believe. Begging, like Nettie and her girl were doing to the cats in the corner. And the brothers, playing, jiving, signifying around the table, begged back. You could beg with words, or without them. Could beg silently, with your thighs, your eyes, your body, perhaps even your back, like he did with Dia minutes ago. Your back. His was turned to his mom's table, but she wasn't there. "This is a man's world." The title of JB's song made him recall Smythe's sermon. "What is man, that Thou art mindful of him?" The black marble bar shone, as did the gleaming black floor. "Clean enough to eat off of," his mom's words about how a kitchen floor should be kept. Rumor was that Johnny owned this place. Who did? Maybe that smiling, round-headed cat did. His mom knew. Maybe *she* did. She came in here enough. Had decorated the joint. Gave it her touch, like their home. Ever so often, this joint was her home— because it had to be. According to James Brown, this is a man's world. Well, *her* world was them, he and his father. She made that choice when she married his father, and bore him, when she stayed. Stayed for what? For who? For the men in her world? Or for herself? He lifted his glass. "Hey Johnny, let me have another." The Bills were threatening to score. "They gon' win this one," Johnny loudly announced, watching the tv as he filled the order. Stan yelled back at the barkeep, "Leave em alone; they play better when you don't watch!" This last comment caught not only Johnny's attention, but that of several patrons. The Bills scored their touchdown. Maybe *they* would still be alive come Christmas. How many wins if they got this one? He didn't know. Didn't follow them as closely this year as in the past. Stan moved toward the TV, closer to the pool table. It was late in the game, and they were winning by a wide margin; this one was wrapped up. When he was little, his father took him to games at War Memorial Stadium. Later, when he was older, he snuck in to a few games at halftime, with the rest of the Cambridge boys. Could always get in free after halftime. The Bills. Buffalo's team. His team. Basically losers, yet winning today. His town, all his life. In fact, turning his attention from the tube to the pool table, he noticed that neither game was close. Cobbs was kickin' Snooks' butt and woofin' about it. Donnie departed earlier. The ladies-in-waiting feigned interest in the pool and football games as they waited for their men-for-the-evening, and perhaps the night, to be done. Watching Nettie, his childhood playmate, long-legged, big-eyed, enduring Nettie, it seemed that he and she were playing similar games, watching lop-sided victories and waiting their turns. This evening, he and Net, old friends, former schoolyard competitors, again played tag. She was "it" first; then he was. Her play, with one of the pool players; and his. He hoped that their respective plays worked. The only difference was that his, for life or death, must work. No, check that, maybe Net's was also. He wished her Godspeed and the luck of their youth.

* * * * *

Rich sensed that the young woman speeding away from the bar was involved with his son. Hearing her tires scream away from the scene, seeing the long black marks they burnt in the street, he was frightened. He took his time, parallel-parking deliberately, easing the big black Lincoln into a space across the street from the club like he eased himself into bed next to Nancy as she slept, awaiting him, though she never admitted it. Because of her message—"At BB's, waiting for you. This is it," he hurried here, but he couldn't rush. He shivered as he strode across the street, carrying his Bible with him, clutching it tightly as he carefully stepped over the black skid marks in the street. Not seeing Stan's Mustang, he hoped this meant that the young lady was returning. If only he arrived earlier, if only Deacon Craig had given him the message sooner, he might have met Nancy, and they could have entered this place together. They needed to do this together. With every crucial event in his son's life, Sheila and the divorce, the loss of track, and Max's death, Stan changed, withdrew a little bit more. Withdrew into what? Nothing very solid, nothing strong. In spite of all the externals, weightlifting and running, different jobs, Stan seemed defeated, like Rich himself felt at times. Standing in front of the tavern, scanning the deserted street, he recalled how crazy Stan was about this girl. He gauged his son's feelings toward a woman, toward any endeavor, by observing Stan and his mother. If something was crucial to Stan, Nancy became, not less important to him, but less of an influence. It was that way with Sheila; it was that way now. And this girl was the reason. Rich was cold, standing out here, waiting for nothing, and they were inside, so he opened the door and entered. He instantly spied the width of Stan's back as he stood at the bar. Johnny's ever-present grin, accompanied by a busy nod, directed him toward a table, Nancy's. Sitting there and taking in the decor, the jungle of greenery, crisp white linen, brass accents and bud vases, all obvious touches of his wife, he looked up, staring at the photos of proud black heroes gracing the walls. Then, through the convex mirror

above the bar, Stan's fixed, granite visage met Rich's eyes and
shook him, like the speakers blasting Brown's song quaked the
joint, begging them to believe, "This is a man's world." A
"man's world," but one that would be empty without a woman.
Rich looked away. He did believe, the booming bass, the twanging guitars, the screaming brass section, and JB's coarse, husky
voice. No, he knew. Knew what would have happened if his
woman left. Was she still his woman? It seemed so. She must be,
for if she wasn't, he was womanless and would remain so for the
duration of his life. There could be no one else for him. When
did he arrive at that conclusion? Just now? Or years, decades
ago? What would he and Stan have done to one another without
her around? Would they have fought it out? Or simply said, "forget you, niggah." Forget father, son, all that, and walked. At
times, Rich wanted to walk. Away in tears, but never looking
back. Again, JB moaned, "This is a man's world." No, James,
Rich thought, it isn't. Not when the men can't see one another
until it's too late. How did she keep them together yet also prevent them from destroying each other? "Air and opportunity"
divided him and his boy. "Air and opportunity," that phrase, was
part of a neighborhood taunt he overheard while watching from
an upstairs window perhaps his son's first fight, a street fight he
could have stopped but chose not to. "Ain't nothing between us
but air and opportunity, and I give you the opportunity to hit
me first." He overheard that dare once, and it stuck. Stuck because it was uttered by a girl, one of those bad little females who
took no mess. That girl, Nettie, Rich forgot her last name, was
in the bar. Was that why the phrase came to mind? "Air and opportunity"—in a man's world. A black man's world? It wasn't
his boy's world. It wasn't the world of his boy's buddies. So
much talent. But so much air, and so little opportunity. Rich desired to overturn the tables, the tv, the bar, and bring his boy

back to him. He wanted to compress the air between them into a ball, one they could throw and catch. Make it into a ballgame, a contest—one more *opportunity* for him and his seed. They played too few games, when there was time for that. Now, there wasn't. Aching from the loudness of the music and hunger, Rich wanted to leave. He wanted, needed, to leave, to change the music; *change* everything: summon Nancy to this chair close beside him so they could enjoy fried chicken dinners and sweet soul music; and invite Stan with his new girl. He wanted to get back Stan's girl; recall her car as with a giant magnet; needed to resketch, reshoot, the vivid, disdainful stare of his son, transform it into a look of affection. But he couldn't sit still any longer; the music wouldn't let him. So Rich rose, leaving his Bible on the table. He walked with trepidation, because he felt doomed to fall to the floor and be unable to rise. He felt like the preacher proclaimed altar call, and he was coming forth, down the aisle, to the feet of Jesus. Jesus was calling him home. Home. Where in the heaven or hell was home, his home? Did he know any longer? What in heaven or hell did he really know? Really believe? He believed the call. And followed it, as though he were dreaming, gliding, going back, past all those years, years marked by the tiles in this black floor. Each step took him back.

* * * * *

Johnny relayed the message to Stan that his mom would return soon. He knew that. She was here. Not simply that Johnny said she would return, but that she never left. He felt her presence. He wanted to leave. She devised a plan and whatever it was, it contradicted his. He could get up now, and leave, but he wished to see what would happen. "Believe I'll run on and see what the end is gonna be." Usually, his father would be singing that or some other sanctified song right now, praying at the altar with the rest of the saints, but his father was here. "Maybe I am one of them," he said to himself, sipping the o.j. And maybe it *was* time to "run on," to see what the end's gonna be, to leave all of this, and do whatever it was all the songs in his head were saying was possible. Go search for the "new world," was what Uncle Marv called it. Why not just exercise the option and get the hell out of dodge? Begin his own search, start all over again, with whatever life he had left, physically and otherwise. Perhaps that was his father's problem. He never searched for the new world, never realized, yeah James, that this is a mother f-ing black man's world, but you gotta make it one.

* * * * *

Nancy was playing her selections and staying out of it. James Brown was right, and wrong. It was crucial that her men learn, today, that this could be their world, maybe not in a big, famous way, but in a small, intimate way, like this bar, or a church, or a bedroom. It could be their world in a way that only they understood, individually and, perhaps, as a family. But she couldn't be in the middle of it, today. With them before, she was never out of it, not really. But now, all she could do was give them this music and let go.

* * * * *

Rest room. This tiny box afforded neither, its small yellow bulb furnishing little light, its hazy mirror offering a dull image. As Rich stared at himself in the rest room mirror, not to comb his hair or wipe his face, but simply to collect himself, Dinah Washington took charge of the air, serenading the room with her signature song, "What A Difference A Day Makes."

Nancy's favorite song. Anybody and everybody acquainted with her knew this. It was a song they sang, played to, danced to—made love to. She figured they conceived Stan to it. He chuckled, remembering his response to her calculated discovery: "What else could it've been to? That's the only song you play." In the song, Dinah told the tale of how a day could make all the difference in one's life and one's love. This song was Nancy's idea. Nancy was here. There were all kinds of rooms in this place, and Nancy was here. But she chose, for whatever reason, to stay out of it, to not be "Nancy to the rescue," solving the situation between them so it's never solved. The singer pinpointed this difference in time, a day; and in place, the Beloved, and was empathic about one thing. "What A Difference A Day Made." Mom used to sing it to him. He knew it by heart. If you asked some folks about this, Dinah's biggest hit, they would misquote the title, substituting "makes" for "made." "Made" was the word. It, this difference, had occurred. His mom sang it to him as a baby, bouncing his little legs to Dinah's sultry song. It wasn't a slow song, nor was it fast. Just steady, like running that last 400 in practice and still feeling strong. A song of affirmation, Dinah sang it straight. His mom was here, in the back control room. He recalled something she said to him last week. "The only difference between your father and me is our method. We've always wanted the same for you. Sometimes I wish he would change, but that's Rich. And you. Two peas, same pod. Big ideas. Both wanting to be up there." She elevated her hand till it stopped when she could reach no higher. "You in love with this new girl? Well, I'm glad you found somebody you can be satisfied with. Your problem is how to be satisfied with yourself, just like your dad." He wished, as Dinah's sweet song dissolved into the air, that he were a musician who could fill this space with sound, his sound. He wanted to dissolve into the air, like music. He wished, as he listened to the song ending, fading

away, that he could inhabit it, dwell within it, and take them
with him, his mom, his father.

* * * * *

He should've stayed out there, watching his child. "Watch as
well as pray." He should've stood next to his son. Only one faucet, the cold, worked. Rich splashed water on his face, wiping it
dry with his hands, and wringing them in the air. Stan was waiting for him, had been waiting for years. Wait—"tarry"— what
the old saints called praying aloud for the Holy Ghost: "Tarry
till ye be endued with power from on high." Hearing Dinah sing
their old song made him think of the old times, courting Nancy,
playing with his young son, "Daddy's be-bop baby." But
"Daddy's be-bop baby" played out, while Nancy weaved worlds
for the boy with stories, stories Rich listened to, to hear what she
was saying, and then turned off. Her stories for the boy seemed
of another world, an unreal world for just the two of them. He
wished, more than once, that the boy were named for him, so
he'd be "little Rich," or "Jr." He wished, more than once, to
steal the boy from her, even though he needed her to raise him if
he, Rich, was going to realize his dreams. But he didn't realize
them. And neither did his son. A day can make a difference,
Dinah. "This day has to," he prayed. "This day has to."

Wiping his face with a paper towel, looking in the dim mirror,
Rich saw the face of his son. He saw his own reflection, but Stan
was there too, in the mirror with him, looking over his shoulder,
staring. So here he was, trapped in a cramped rest room waiting
for something— someone?—to tell him what to do. What was
Nancy's motive for bidding them here? What was Stan going to
do? Was there a clue here, in this rest room, that would help
him? He knelt, like at the altar or beside his bed, because it was

habit, custom; and what else could he do? It was tough kneeling down, prostrating himself on the cold, black floor. His knees hurt from its hardness. He bent down, bowing, so that his forearms helped support him. He closed his eyes, and the darkness of the tiny room became darker. He barely heard the music now. It didn't exist, or it did, but it was suspended, as were they all: his wife, son, the rest of the barroom, the world. It was just he and God. He and his Lord. A Lord, right now, he didn't know if he could reach. He prayed.

"Father, give me wisdom and guidance. I don't know, really, why I'm here. But I want to do your will. Help me. I need you."

Then he began to cry, as a one might do at a funeral or a christening. He cried, as a father for his son, for his failures as a father, as a man. He didn't touch the tears. Opening his eyes, looking into the cramped darkness, he rose cautiously, holding onto the smooth porcelain sink, gripping it, using both his hands so he wouldn't fall. Trembling, he rose steadily to his full height. He brushed himself off, but he didn't bother looking in the mirror. As he entered the barroom, Nancy was spinning Freddie Hubbard's rendition of "Father and Son." Hubbard's trumpet horn seemed a clarion call, like the sounding of the last trump. Not noticing him, Stan shouted above the music, to the woman across the barroom, "Net, how come we never did that date? You know you been promising me since I returned home. We used to have a crush on each other. What happened?" Grinning, he shouted above the music to the men huddled over the pool table. "Hey Cobbs, when are you and I gonna run some ball, man? We haven't played in what, ten years? You still think you can beat me? You couldn't back then, chump."

Amidst the chaos of the pool game and television and Stan's shouts, Rich began walking toward his son. Nobody noticed him, but he wavered as he walked. His legs felt heavy, and they weren't his legs anymore, but were controlled by the man-boy across the room, whose broad, black, muscular back forbade him to come any closer. Nancy was playing "Father and Son" on purpose. She summoned them here on purpose. That purpose was linked with this walk, with his son at the end of this brief journey. "Walk by faith, and not by sight." Rich felt that he was taking his first steps, or his last, and all eyes were riveted on him. It was like walking down the aisle at one's wedding, when the simple act of walking poses questions: can I do this? Should I do this? But then, he realized, no eyes were on him. The brown eyes and faces within the black room were focused on his son. He was invisible. And so were they all, except for his son. Reaching him, leaning against the rich black wood of the bar, Rich spoke to his son's back.

"Son, let's talk."

In slow motion, Stan turned around to face him. They were close enough to touch. Stan was taller than him by two, three inches, but he seemed to tower over Rich; he spoke down, as from a perch. "Leave me alone. I didn't come here for you. I came for mom."

"Your mom, where is she?" Rich shot an eye toward Johnny, hoping for an answer, but the barkeep ignored him.

"She's here. But it's too late." Stan reached into his bag and snatched out a gun, Rich's own gun. Pulling the trigger, he blasted the white plaster ceiling, shattering the syncopated interplay of Hubbard's trumpet and Wayne Shorter's sax. Chunks of ceiling plummeted to the floor like hailstones. Everyone in the joint screamed, cursed, jumped. The smiles which his questions elicited now vanished from the faces of his friends. Tears streamed down Candy's frightened, round, caramel-colored cheeks. The pool players stared, their cues upraised like the African spears of warriors. Johnny peered into the one-way mirror.

Nettie hollered across the room like it was a vast chasm. "Stan, this is crazy! I don't know if this is between you and your family, but don't have the rest of us involved in yalls' mess. Let us out of here first."

"What's crazy, Net? This bar, all of us here, or me shooting this gun?" He waved it at them, gesturing the group away from the black metal door. "Don't move, hear me? Don't try for the door or the phone, either. That includes you," he said to his father, motioning with the weapon for Rich to join the group now congregated behind the pool table. Rich didn't move.

Some in the bar shouted curses; another screamed, "Bum-rush the fool. He can't shoot us all."

"Stan, son," Johnny implored, "stop this nonsense and let's us talk."

"Yawl, he's not gon do nothin'," Nettie yelled. "Johnny, go call the cops," she shouted to the barkeep who still stared into the one-way mirror.

"You're wrong, Net, you're wrong," Stan replied. "I will hurt somebody. I have nothing to lose." He addressed the one-way mirror. "Mom, I have cancer. And I'm probably going to die soon. That's one of the reasons I returned home. I almost told you the other day. And it hurts, you know? But I really didn't come home to fight the cancer, mom. I came back to fight for you. To maybe help you get it together or just leave, die to each other, you know, like me and Sheila. She was right. When you walk out, baby, just walk. And don't leave a forwarding address. Besides, I've lived with cancer all my life. All my life," he paused, then continued, "I've been sick because, like my father, I could never be perfect." Elevating the gun overhead, he punctuated his statement with a gunshot into the photo of "four de hard way." It crashed to the floor, bits of glass exploding like fireworks, causing his father to shield his face with his hands. Could he shoot him, Stan wondered. Or himself? How long could he keep his friends at bay? Soon they would realize his gun held just a few more bullets; and he, so little strength, to continue holding them at bay. Soon they would rush him, or call the cops. He spoke to the mass huddled by the door. "Nettie, Cobbs, all yall can leave. I don't care if yall call the cops or whatever. It'll all be over by the time they get here." He watched as they quickly gathered their things, scurrying about, snatching up their belongings like on a mad shopping spree. As they did so, they maintained distrusting eyes on him. When they were kids, romping through rusty, dusty, working-class streets together, they would've trusted him. They might've double-dared him, as kids do. If it were a squirt pistol, they might've begun to run around, chanting words like, "can't catch me, can't catch me." Now, however, their troubled faces displayed how deeply they feared that whatever he caught was contagious, dangerous, deadly. He felt the same regarding them. He didn't want to end up like them, settling for small plays, happy with mediocrity. "Shoulda, coulda, woulda," an anthem of his people, here and elsewhere. But he loved em. "Yall get on, I apologize for scaring yall," he spoke to their backs, to the massive black metal door, and Nettie's face as she turned, mouthing a silent goodbye as she left.

He didn't know what to do with Johnny, but then, Johnny was like family. His mom made her presence felt through the air, through sound. The staccato, tentative yet forceful fingering of Hassan, "To Inscribe." Tentative because he finally received a chance. Forceful because first chances could also be last. Stan loved this cut. It reminded him of why he came. The race wasn't over. If anything, he was trailing, and had hit, hard, the invisible wall every runner encounters at least once. The music, the room, encompassed him, like a crowded stadium. He was straining, pushing himself, but still he was trailing. He wanted to sit down and quit; he didn't care about finishing. He wanted to create his own finish line, draw it, with the broken bits of ceiling, a heavy white line on the littered black floor. He hoped, like with his mom, Dia could read his heart and mind, and right now was turning around her car, making a u-turn in the middle of some street to come get him. He should have chased after Dia's car, run it down, like it was one last runner between himself and the tape.

His father's words broke in, "Have you gotten treatment?"

Against his mind, Stan answered, "yes."

"Where?"

"Everywhere, every damned where. Really, I've been treated by some of the best physicians. I've studied this disease."

"What's the prognosis?"

"The prognosis is, was, when I left Harrisburg, that I was going to die soon. In months. I feel I've prolonged my life by . . . ."

"By what?" And now, Stan noticed that his father, who earlier had been stationary, was now directly in front of him, like a tape at the end of a race. One step, and he'd break through it. His father was eyeing him, eyeing the gun. Johnny had vanished, perhaps to call the cops or perhaps to wait with his mom in the control room, where Johnny also kept his guns.

Stan was proud of his mom. She stayed out of it. But what was it? Nothing was resolved. He missed Dia. He didn't want to shoot anyone, and he didn't want to die. He didn't even know how to answer his father's question, if he should recite the litany of "cures" he investigated, the opinions he sought, on how to beat the disease. *He* wanted to ask his father questions, to put him on the witness stand, the judgement seat.

But then, Stan thought he detected a familiar sound, a familiar screeching and car door slamming, and looked toward the door. His father leapt on him, tackling him, reaching around his son's body. Like two drunkards vainly attempting to dance together, they stumbled hard into the black bar. Then they fell to the floor, entangled in one another's arms, fighting for a gun neither wished to shoot. With one hand, his left, Stan held the gun. This hand and arm were underneath his father's torso. His other arm was wrapped around his father, pinning *his* arms as best he could to prevent him from grabbing the gun. Close to him like this, Stan could count the hairs on his father's greying head. Or, if he relinquished his hold on the gun, he could shake the old man like a child would a stuffed animal. Or, if he let go of the gun, he could turn his father's body and hit him repeatedly. "I hope you learn that people can only love you the way life teaches them to," the words of his mother, last week, about his father. His father, whose eyes were the color of blood, pled softly, "Let me up, son, please, let me up." He wasn't going to. He had him. He could end this anytime he wished. Or he could try to hold him forever. He could use his superior strength to maneuver his father into the jagged edges of broken glass, to cut him, hurt him. Rays of light filtered through the black Venetian blinds, casting shadow stripes, like prison bars, across his father's strained, wrinkled face. Bright shards of glass, glimmering in the light, surrounded his father's head like a ghastly crown. His always-clean old man was dirty, his slick black wool suit was ripped, torn. As Stan gazed on his weary, beaten father, looking old for the first time, the old man's eyes were closed, but his mouth was moving. Stan couldn't make out the words. His father wasn't moving, resisting anymore.

Years ago, Nancy answered the question, "when do you cease being a parent, when your child becomes grown, when he's gone, when you've given him to another woman to have and hold, when you've sent him out with your blessing?" But she never sent him out. The closest was now. Every minute of his life, she carried him, as though he were yet in her womb, unborn, perhaps never to be born, never to take physical leave of her body. But he had, and so she carried him, from day one in her heart and soul. But not now. Now, she sent him away, paradoxically, into the embrace of his father, black man wrapped around black man—but she owned neither of them now. Now, right now, she relinquished all of the wishes she held for them. There were days when she cried for them to cling to each other. Yet when her husband tackled her son, she yelled, "Let go!" at the top of her lungs, to drown out Hassan's incessant piano. The moment they hit, she yelled "let go," the opposite of what she lived for. She fought, prayed, *laid herself down*, became their doormat, so that they, as a family, *would not* let go of one another, so that they would cleave to each other, like the Bible said. But she screamed "let go," to pierce through the sound-proof barrier. They couldn't hear her, but she yelled "let go!" from the center of her soul, her womanhood, where she loved the man and carried the child who were entangled in dirty, dusty blackness, black running shoes, black Sunday suit, on the black marble floor. Had she a broom, she'd beat them apart, but all she held was one of Johnny's guns which she dared not fire. She needn't worry about Johnny harming Stan. Stan was the closest he had left to a son. He simply followed her lead. They didn't exchange words, just stark black faces which agreed to wait, to allow this drama to play itself out. When the crew departed, Johnny locked the door, whispering to Nettie on her way out, "Yawl let us handle this. None a yawl call the cops on my boy, hear?"

Later, Stan would wonder why he didn't simply toss the gun away, scoot it across the floor, but at the time, he knew: Dia. He thought Dia was about to enter, and he didn't want the gun to accidentally discharge, and possibly harm her. But when she didn't come through the big black door, or pound rapidly on it—did Johnny lock it?—he held onto the grey gun like it was Dia, or all the women he ever loved, all the men he claimed as brothers; like holding onto that gun would gather together his loved ones: bring back Dia, resurrect Max, or cure his cancer. With one hand, Stan gripped the gun securely yet lightly, like it was a baton. He was running anchor, and Max passed the baton to him, thrust it urgently into his sweaty, nervous hand, because they were trailing in the race, and it was on Stan to bring them home victoriously. Max slapped the baton into his outstretched hand so that, for a moment, their hands, joined by the stick, became one hand, and the stick became a bridge between him and brother Max. Once he received the baton from his bro, his perspiring, glistening bro, he ran like the wind, not simply because there was a race to be won, but also because he loved the man from whom he snatched the stick. The baton was their lives, a link between them that he, alone, carried on—an umbilical cord which, once severed, became a stronger tie than ever, a cord which couldn't be cut by time or space or death itself.

Then, again, Stan thought he detected her footsteps. Thought, wished, that his prayers were answered, and Dia ceased being Dia—for a moment, a day—like in Dinah's song, and returned to rescue him. He glanced toward the door, anticipating her entrance. Then his father stole away the gun. Not with strength, but with speed. Stan reacted, too, believing his woman was coming through the door, hoping that she was striding toward the door like an Olympic speed walker; yet praying that she wasn't, like a child beseeching Santa to not come after all, but to ride on past with the anxiously awaited gift. His free hand swept through air the moment his father grabbed the gun. He was running anchor, and the baton was his next. Simultaneously, like a good baton pass, where hand and hand reach together, and become, for a twinkling, one, his hand reached his father's as the elder's snatched and triggered cold steel. Stan's hand reached and slapped it, like he would do the back of a joyous teammate. Slapped it, like on a baby's butt to test for life. "Dad!"—his hand slapped the weapon so that the line of its fire changed . . . .

Rich held his bleeding son. "Call an ambulance!" "I've got him, I've got him," Rich snapped at Nancy as she burst around the bar toward them. "Help me, Nan, you brace him from the other side," he said softly, to his crying, kneeling wife. She gently placed her arms under their son's back. Because of the way Stan turned toward the sound, because of the way they were entangled on the floor, the bullet penetrated Stan's side. "Johnny! Get my keys, they're over there. Pull my car up to the door. If the ambulance doesn't come in a minute we'll take it." Rich took off his suit jacket and tied it tightly around the wound to try to stop the bleeding.

* * * * *

He didn't die. But the doctors said, "he'll never walk again." During the months in the hospital, after a while, his life reached a regularity. His folks came daily; and Leah and folks from the neighborhood came frequently, especially Johnny and Nettie. Dia came twice; once during the first week, when he was asleep; and once, before she moved, but she "didn't have an address yet," and she'd "be in touch." Two months in the hospital allowed him time to think and write. In terms of writing, Ton's idea about seven letters worked. Stan was able to finally reach KK. KK and Ton arrived together to visit him. The conclusion of all seven letters was the same:

I believe I will walk again, but I'm just beginning to realize, since I can't now, since my legs have no strength, the strength in the rest of me. I'm still fighting the cancer. Whatever I was doing didn't hurt, the doctors say. Now, I'm just not fighting it alone.

I've always felt that the most crucial identities are those into which we are born: Stanford Thompson; male; black. The next level of identities has always been those into which we, or circumstances, put ourselves: Four de hard way; college grad; freelance writer (smile).

On each level, the key is learning to live, not with, but *within* the identity while simultaneously living *without* it. I'm learning this with my condition. God's love and mine.

Sincerely,
Stanford.

* * * * *

The airport was busy. The noises of the busy terminal blasted, like the rushing would-be passengers, from every direction. Sky-caps, brothers all, steered their golf carts carrying the aged and infirmed like they were sportscars on the street. A few business-men were half-slumped in padded seats, seemingly oblivious to the pretty, fast-walking stewardesses wheeling their luggage to work, or from it. Others, those who experienced easier days, toasted that ease at the terminal's pubs. Two well-dressed young men in the corner of one of the pubs gazed out the window at technicians readying a jet for flight. They'd roomed together during the previous weekend, like old times.

Ton turned to his companion. "What time your plane leave again?"

"8:10," KK replied. "Man, I wish Son was comin' with me now. Said my hospital could help with his therapy."

"Didn't he say he was coming to Accra as soon as he gets better?"

"Yeah, asked me to talk with my brother-in-law 'bout a teaching job. That mothafucka' think he gon walk again." K said wryly. "But he is gettin' damn good with that chair."

"Yes, Dr. Karikari," Ton agreed, feigning seriousness, then finished his drink, a scotch and water, and motioned to the bartender for refills.

"I'm glad we came to see Son an' all, but it's still kinda hard for me to accept he can't jump out that chair and run a 400," K said, downing his drink, seemingly to emphasize his words; or to catch up with his friend. "But I guess he'll be alright, all those pretty women visiting his ass."

"Yeah," Alton looked down at his drink.

"Man, that cat's a bigger celebrity in Buffalo now than when we used to run." K reached for his newly set up drink.

"We both still got some time, wanna get something to eat?" Alton pulled out his wallet. "My treat. You've bought since we've been here."

"I wanna get drunk. And then laid. By that woman right-tt there." K nodded at a tall, tight-skirted black woman who sauntered by. He slid off his barstool, leaving his unfinished drink.

Alton followed, taking one last gulp from his glass. "You take any of the clothes Son was giving away?" Alton spoke to K's back.

"Naw, man, I can't wear his stuff." K weaved his way through the congested bar to the main thoroughfare.

"I took a couple of things, I'm not gonna wear 'em, K, just keep 'em. Most of it's old UB track stuff. Mementos."

Having reached the walkway, K halted, turning to Alton as though what was on his mind must be articulated before any further more motion. "Mrs. T a nice lady. Said she happy they tryin' to get it together, Stan and his dad. That mothafucka must feel awful, though. His own son. Must feel . . . . "

"Like we do, K, like we do." Alton stopped too; while K

mumbled more about the events of Stan's accident, he studied K's African, tribal scar-marked face for a sign, something that would make him feel better not just about Son's cancer and paralysis, but about leaving their buddy behind. He missed, they missed, their times together; and now this. Yet he wondered, did you miss a friend whom you had not seen for years *differently*, after such an accident? Especially when you missed them already? Maybe you just missed the possibilities.

"Son was bleeding in his daddy's arms." K spit out onto the floor the shreds of a toothpick. "What he say, 'my hands were the first and almost the last to touch his life, but I failed to touch him throughout?'"

"Yeah, but I'm tired of replaying it," Alton replied, punching K's arm. "Let's walk, man."

K remained still except to swing his multi-colored, African print shoulder bag from around his neck, and drop it to the floor, hitting a rushing passer-by in the process. Ignoring the man's stare of annoyance, he knelt next to it, fishing inside.

Ton looked around. "Which way you want to go? Can probably find something either way." In each direction there seemed to be endless corridor.

K rose, having brought out of his bag a relay baton with a worn, frayed white ribbon tied around it. "Remember this?" He waved it at Alton. "Son said something about passing on what was good from the past. Said since I wouldn't take nothing else for me to give this to my son, when I get one." K grinned for the first time since Richard dropped them off at the airport. "No way I wasn't gonna take it."

Alton studied the wooden cylinder; one of his hands moved the baton in K's so he could read what was on the ribbon. Written in black magic marker was: "'77, FOUR DE HARD WAY, #1." Ton spoke softly, reverently, to his friend, "The Nationals."

"Go down to the next gate. See, #33?" K pointed down the corridor to a sign. "Go down dere and be ready. I'm gon sprint it to you, and 'den we'll just keep on going. Stop when we want to."

Alton returned K's grin as he took off in a trot toward the mark.

The End.